Bad for You

USA TODAY & WALL STREET JOURNAL BESTSELLING AUTHOR

CHARITY FERRELL

Editing: Editing 4 Indies

prologue

NAUTICA

"WE SHOULDN'T BE DOING THIS," he says, the words strained as they fall from his lips.

He slowly slides his cock inside me, his actions not matching his words, and heat rips through my blood with his first thrust.

"I know," I whisper. "But nobody has to know."

Holding back a grin, I mentally throw my hands up in victory.

Us together is what I've wanted for years.

Is this a one-night stand?

I hope not, but I'm too terrified to ask.

I stare at him. His thick lips are parted, and his eyes are hungry as he pounds inside me with force.

This man.

This fucking man.

He's my obsession.

And me?

I'm a foolish girl.

Like so many tragic, love-sick fools before me, I've fallen for a man I can't have. I knew before his soft lips grazed mine, before I fell in his bed, before I allowed him to touch and taste every inch of me that he would never be mine.

But that didn't stop me.

Take my advice.

Never fall for your brother's best friend.

one

NAUTICA

"YOU BETTER HAVE a good as fuck explanation why you're here."

Oh shit.

Even in the rambunctious college coed-filled bar, there's no mistaking who the husky voice behind me belongs to. It's haunted me for years, taken too many parts in my self-induced orgasms, and ruined every chance I've had of loving another man.

I drop the cash in my hand in what seems like slow motion.

Thud.

I hear my pulse thrash against my ears.

Thud.

Out of every damn bar on campus, he had to come here tonight.

Go fucking figure.

There goes my night of craziness before I head home for the holidays.

The bartender slides my drink in front of me, scoops up the fallen cash, and meanders off to help his next customer, leaving me in dread. I stay frozen in place, debating whether to hop over the bar and make a run for it.

I take a pass on that idea. He'll chase after me, and my embarrassing high school track record tells me I'll lose.

"Nautica," he barks, causing me to jump. "Turn your ass around and look at me before I toss you over my shoulder and drag you out of here."

He's not bluffing. He'll do it and most likely cause a scene to teach me a lesson.

I take a long gulp of my too-strong drink to gain some liquid courage and slowly pivot around on my heels. I yelp when the vodka soda gets ripped from my hand. He lifts it to his smirking lips and chugs it down tauntingly.

Asshole.

"What the fuck?" I snap, gaining the attention of the surrounding crowd. "Rude much?" I make a grab for my now empty glass but fall short when he holds it higher than my five-foot-three frame.

The jackass has a good eight inches on me.

"Do you mind?" I ask.

"No, I don't fucking mind. This is the last time I'll ask. What the hell are you doing here?" His devious blue eyes level down on me, making me even more nervous. He crosses his arms over his muscular chest and leans back on his heels, waiting for my reply.

I'm trying my damnedest to keep up with my pissed-off attitude, but my attraction to him mixed with the alcohol flowing through my veins is altering my mind.

I lick my lips. His jet-black hair is slicked back with gel. Not in a geekish way—more of an *I'm trying to look casual but still get girls to drop their panties in a second* kind of way. A black flannel button-up is thrown over his white V-neck tee, and his ripped jeans hang low on his hips.

Damn, I want this man.

I part my lips, certain I'm going to salivate at any moment. This is what happens when you're around the guy you've been obsessing over for years. You pant like a fucking dog in heat.

Bracken Casey.

He's my brother's best friend and the guy designated as my babysitter while I'm away attending Kansas University. He'd never been given that job title had my older brother, Simon, known all the dirty things I wanted to do to him.

I ignore the curious stares pointed our way and gesture to the crowded bar. "What does it look like I'm doing?" I hiss. "The same damn thing you are. I'm having fun." I attempt to squeeze past him. "So, if you'll excuse me while I go do that."

He grips my waist, his nails roughly biting into my skin, and stops me. His sharp gaze roams to my left side and then to my right. My eyes shoot to the floor, fully aware of what is coming next.

"Who the fuck are you here having fun with?" he questions. "From the looks of it, you seem like some desperate, naïve chick alone in a bar waiting for some guy to date rape her."

My eyes don't leave the beer-splattered ground. "Macy," I lie.

Okay, I halfway lie.

I came here with my best friend, but she ditched me fifteen minutes ago in the arms of the last guy who bought her a drink before heading back to our dorm. She'd suggested I call Bracken and ask to crash at his place or come back in a few hours if I don't want to hear her getting screwed.

His chilly fingers wrap around my chin to lift my head, forcing me to look at him. "So … where the fuck is your little roommate then?" He makes an annoying show of looking around the room.

Shit. Shit. Shit.

"She, uh ... had to run back to our dorm real quick." I'm not fast on my toes in the lying department, which is why I never got to do illegal shit in high school. Simon always tripped me up when I couldn't keep my stories straight.

His lower lip snarls as his face twists in anger. "She had to run back to your dorm real quick?" he repeats slowly. "The bitch did it again, didn't she? I'm going to strangle her."

I stumble forward when he snags my elbow and drags me across the room to the back of the bar.

"I told you to quit hanging out with that ho."

I'd planned to call him asking if I could stay at his apartment, but I wasn't ready to call it a night yet. I wanted to enjoy one last drink before taking a cab back to his place, so he wouldn't know I'd been here.

Unfortunately, just like my roomie, that plan is long gone.

I jerk out of his hold. "First off, don't call my best friend a ho."

"She fucking ditches you nonstop to ride douchebags' cocks. I'll call her a ho and every other name in the fucking book if I want. Swear to God, you're not rooming with her next year. I don't give a shit if you're stuck with some chick who eats her boogers and picks her ass. It won't be Macy."

"She has a high sexual appetite. Don't use that against her or try to act like your friends"—I snort—"or that you're any better. Just because you all have tiny weasel dicks instead of a vagina doesn't make you superior."

For years I've watched him and my brother recycle girlfriend after girlfriend. Or hookup after hookup, considering they think a committed relationship is the equivalency of having your balls on a chain.

He laughs, but his face turns serious. "Now, I can't speak for my friends, but my cock is definitely far from being tiny. Don't mistake me for one of those frat boys you keep wasting your time with."

A smile builds along my lips. "Prove it to me then."

Excitement trickles up my spine like a lit match at my challenge. The mood shifts. I lock my eyes on him, but he averts his gaze, refusing to look at me.

I fell in love with this man before I knew what the word love meant. He'd stolen my heart the first time I saw him. He was the kid down the street who rode his bike over the day we moved in. The box in my hand had tumbled to the ground when he slammed on the brakes and hopped off his bicycle. The heel of his Converse sneakers punched down on the metal kickstand. He shoved his hands in the pockets of his jeans and came my way with a bright smile on his face. Even at twelve, the boy was a charmer.

The night of his graduation party, I'd embarrassingly and drunkenly confessed my undying love for him. I snuck out of my house with Macy, and we crashed the party. He blew me off, making it crystal clear I was his best friend's little sister. That was it. He didn't and would never see me that way.

I ended the night crying in his passenger seat while he took me home and then puked in the floorboard of his truck as a last goodbye. He snuck me back into my house, tucked me in, and disappeared like a stranger in the night. We've never brought it up. It's like it never happened.

"How did you even get in here?" he asks, choosing to ignore my comment.

He has a habit of doing that, and it pisses me off. I know my flirting annoys him, but I'm a determined woman. Eventually, I'll get Bracken to fall for me ... or at least, fall in my bed.

"The same way you did," I answer. "I walked through the front door." I groan when he gives me a hard look. "Fine. My ID."

"Your ID.?"

I nod.

"That's weird, considering your ID says you're only fucking nineteen. I know this place is strict on checking that shit too. So spill, Nautica."

"I have a fake."

"Where the fuck did you score a fake?"

"That's none of your business."

Macy dated a guy who hooked us up with them a few months ago. She slept with him a few times, slipped him twenty bucks, and we took our first trip to the liquor store twelve hours later.

"It's time for you to go." He grabs my arm again and practically drags me through the crowd. We stop at a crowded table where Jasper, his roommate, and a few other guys are sitting.

"Well, look who it is. I was wondering where the hell you ran off to," Jasper says when he notices us. "I assumed it was for some pussy. But not this off-limits pussy." He looks me up and down with a smart-ass grin on his face and laughs when I flip him off.

Jasper is a head-full-of-blond-hair pretty boy. He reminds me of your stereotypical college guy who plays tennis and spends his daddy's money on too much booze and women.

"Who do we have here?" a drunken voice asks.

I look over at a guy I don't recognize sitting next to Jasper. He has shaved brown hair and is wearing thick-framed hipster glasses. I cringe at the overeager look on his face.

I let out a grunt when Bracken snags me around the hips and pushes me behind his powerful body.

"Hands off, asshole," he warns, spit flying from his mouth. His voice thunders with authority. "She's my best friend's little sister. She's off-limits, and I mean it."

"Touch her, and he'll kick your ass, man," Jasper says, cutting in.

I step out from behind Bracken and give him a dirty look.

"I tried once and got a fist to the face," Jasper goes on before pointing at his crooked nose. "Almost fucking broke this beauty."

"I have to take her home or ... somewhere. I'll be back," Bracken tells them.

"I can't go home for a few hours ... or possibly until morning," I say, stopping him.

"Then you can hang out in my truck until Macy is finished being fucked."

"Dude, quit being a fun sucker," Jasper calls out. "Let her hang with us. You can keep an eye on her here. You think she wants to go home and deal with that shit?" He signals to the empty stool next to him and then to me. "Sit your ass down, get a drink, and let's have some fun."

I hop on the barstool before Bracken drags me out of here. Jasper winks at me.

"Simon doesn't hear about this," Bracken says, taking the seat next to me. "And your ass is drinking water."

"Absolutely not," I argue.

Jasper jumps off his stool. "So you don't get your panties in a bunch, roomie, I'll get her a drink," he tells Bracken. He glances over at me. "Any special requests?"

"Whatever is fine. I'm not picky," I answer.

He claps his hands. "Thatta girl. It's shot time, ladies and gentlemen!" He salutes us before heading over to the bar.

"I take it you have no place to crash tonight?" Bracken asks.

"Unless I want to listen to my best friend get railed, then nope. She suggested I call you and crash at your place. I asked a few friends on our floor, but their rooms are full."

"Hate to break it to you, but so is our place. I can drop you off at the homeless shelter a few blocks away. They have fresh sheets and hot meals."

I smack his shoulder. "Very funny, asshole."

He grins, giving me a view of his straight white teeth. "My place it is?"

I nod. "And I'm getting your bed. Jasper's bedroom was fucking disgusting the last time I stayed over. He had condoms, *used condoms*, sitting on his nightstand only a few inches from my pillow." I cringe, disgust rising up my throat as I remember how I dry-heaved at the sight of them. I ended up grabbing a blanket from Bracken's room and sleeping over Jasper's comforter, trying to do everything in my power to keep my body from touching anything. "How disgusting is that? The trashcan was only three steps away. I counted!"

"Oh, quit being a spoiled princess. Be grateful he was gone, and you didn't have to sleep on the couch."

"It would've been more sanitary than condom city."

"I'm not so sure I can agree with that statement. Jasper has allowed a lot of his friends to sleep on that thing. Not to mention, he fucks all the girls he doesn't deem worthy of his bed on it. Now, considering we both know how low his standards are, which one would you prefer?"

I frown. He has a point.

I straighten my back up. "How about you be a gentleman for once and let me sleep in your bed?"

He shakes his head. "The only time a chick is allowed to stay in my bed is if my cock is in her mouth or between her legs. Otherwise, that shit doesn't happen. I don't share my bed or have sleepovers. You've known me long enough to know that."

Every inch of my skin tingles. I close my eyes and imagine what it would be like to be that girl. The one who has his cock in her mouth or between her legs.

That lucky girl.

I'm jealous of her.

I quiver, hoping he can't see the blush rising along my cheeks. I take a minute to reply. "You know I'm not like most chicks you let in your bedroom."

"Trust me, I'm fully aware of that."

"It's settled. I get your bed."

"No. Consider yourself lucky I *might* not tell Simon what Macy pulled tonight. I hate secrets, and it's happened too many times."

My back stiffens. Neither my brother nor Bracken are big Macy fans.

"Please. You know how he is. He'll put me on lockdown. Shit, he'll make me drop out. You know he doesn't like Macy. If you tell him what's going on, it'll be the screw that nails down the coffin."

"Perfect. I'd be honored to provide the hammer."

Jasper comes back with our drinks and hands me one before Bracken gets the chance to confiscate it. Everyone at the table counts to three before tipping their glasses up. I almost gag at the taste of the hard alcohol but still gulp it down so I don't look too much like a rookie—like I don't belong. I don't want Bracken thinking I can't handle my alcohol and make me leave.

Jasper slams his empty shot glass down and looks over at me. "Nautica, I like you and all, but you can't have my bed tonight. My girl gets back in town in the morning. She'll slit my throat and gut me if I have another chick in my bed."

"Dude, you need to leave Tori's crazy ass. She scares the shit out of me," another guy says. Lyle. I recognize him. He's a regular at their apartment. He went to high school with Jasper.

"The crazier they are, the better in bed," Jasper explains, a sly grin taking over his face.

Bracken grunts. "I'd rather have mediocre sex with a sane woman than have a girl who takes her anger out on my car with a baseball bat. I'll pass on that shit any day. I like my pussy without the crazy."

"That's what you say now because you've never had crazy pussy. You just wait until you get one," Jasper fires back.

I look over at Bracken. "I guess that means I get your bed, and you can couch it," I say, interrupting their conversation. I don't want to hear Jasper talking about what type of pussy Bracken should have any longer, or jealousy might eat me alive.

"Sorry, babe, but there's a problem with your little plan," Jasper says. "My cousin, George, is crashing with us tonight. He's visiting from back home." He looks at the guy sitting across from us. "Although, I'm sure he wouldn't mind sharing."

George looks nearly thirty. His brown hair is in a ponytail that's nearly as long as mine, and scruff is scattered along his jawline. He only shrugs his shoulders and takes a long draw of his beer. He definitely isn't interested in me, and I'm definitely not interested back.

"Shut the fuck up, Jasper," Bracken grumbles, narrowing his eyes at him. "Nautica, you can sleep on the floor in my room."

I frown. "I think you meant to say you're sleeping on the floor and giving me your bed."

He shakes his head in response.

"Holy shit, dude," Jasper says, choking back a laugh. "You're going to do her that dirty?" He throws his head back and howls in laughter. "Hell yeah, that's my fucking boy. I wish I could be as chill as you. You act like a complete dickhead, and chicks still line up to give you their pussy."

My eyes shoot over to Bracken. He tightens his fingers around his beer bottle and looks away.

Bracken hooking up with random girls regularly isn't a secret. Jealousy ate at me like acid when I'd spot him leading those hookups to our guest bedroom. Eventually, I stopped going out of my bedroom when my brother threw parties.

I had been an envious fifteen-year-old girl who hadn't hit puberty yet. I wasn't anything like those women. They were gorgeous with big boobs and hair styled perfectly. I despised every single one of them. I still do.

"I swear to God, I need to find a new roommate," Bracken says, giving Jasper a dirty look.

"I'm available," I call out, holding up my hand and giving him a grin. "You said I needed to leave Macy. That's perfect."

"You aren't getting my room, sweetheart," Jasper says.

"You moving in with me wasn't what I was referring to," Bracken fires back. "Not happening."

Jasper gets up and returns with another round of shots. This one is easier to get down. So is the next one.

I lose track of the number of drinks I've consumed. My stomach rumbles with all the crazy mixtures floating around in it.

I'm going to regret this in the morning, but tonight all I can think about is the fact I'm going back to Bracken's place and sleeping in his room.

two

BRACKEN

I GRIP my beer as I lean back on my barstool and watch Nautica. It's what I've done since she sat her sexy ass down on that stool and made herself comfortable.

When I spotted her standing at the bar earlier, wearing that short dress, I nearly lost it. Thoughts of her getting drunk and going home with a random guy ran through my mind.

She has no damn reason to be here. She needs to get her ass back to her dorm room and read a book or some shit.

We're having a good-ass time, and the uneasiness of her being here has faded. It's like we're two friends hanging out and having drinks ... except my dick is hard as I look at her. Us going back to my house later scares yet also excites me.

It's going to be one long-ass night.

I ignore Jasper's elbow hits and comments when women walk past our table—their tits close to falling from their tops as they smile at me. I don't give a shit about them tonight. I barely pay them a glance before my attention returns to Nautica.

There's no better view than her. She rivals every woman here, winning every single damn round. She's gorgeous tonight, and I have a love-hate relationship with her dress. It hugs every perfect curve she's working with. It's short, *too damn short,* but I appreciate the view it's giving me of her tanned legs. I'll be thinking about her ass in it for days.

Her black hair is thrown into a loose ponytail at the top of her head, exposing her swan-like neck and angelic face. Those thick strands would fit perfectly in my fist to pull on as I glide my hard cock into her.

I look away and chug the rest of my beer, hoping it will drown away the thoughts of bending her over that stool and taking her right here.

She's off-limits. Hands off. Remember that.

That rule is easier said than done. She's beautiful, perfection, and thinks I want nothing to do with her. She's so damn wrong.

I'm not the only one with my attention on her. There's no missing the appreciative glances other men are giving her. I narrow my eyes and shoot them silent warnings to stay the fuck away. She's not going home with any of those fuckers. She's going home with me.

A few hours later, I cut her off from accepting any more drinks from Jasper. The guy drinks alcohol like a fish does water. There's no way Nautica can keep up unless she wants to spend the night hugging the porcelain throne, and I'm not in the mood to play caretaker tonight.

My mind wanders back to the night she crashed my graduation party. She drunkenly confessed she loved me and had for years. I gripped my steering wheel, listening to her mutter all the dirty things she wanted to do with me, shocked I didn't crash my truck. The way her face fell when I told her I didn't see her that way killed me. I lied, and she rewarded me by puking in my truck.

That night still haunts me. It's the night it killed me to say no to her.

"You ready to go?" I ask her. I run my hand along her bare arm to get her attention and grin when goose bumps pop up. I love that my touch affects her.

"Are you ready?" she replies, looking away from Jasper to me.

I nod. "I'm fucking beat."

We finish our drinks and call cabs. Jasper and his cousin hop in one car. Nautica joins me in the other.

"Did you have fun tonight?" I ask.

"I did," she answers. Her cheeks flush underneath the dim light as she grins from ear to ear.

I feel the heat of her body when she moves in closer to nudge me with her elbow.

"I told you it wouldn't be so bad letting me stay. I'm fun," she says.

She clips a strand of hair falling from her ponytail behind her ear. I blink—telling myself to quit staring at her tits and thinking about pulling up that dress and fucking her in this back seat.

Shit, I'll tip the driver extra.

For years, fucking years, I've been trying to convince myself she's not attractive, not my type, but I've only been lying to myself. I'm more attracted to her than anyone. She's flawless in my eyes. She has the perfect body, a laid-back personality, and a heart of gold.

If Simon weren't my best friend, I would've already been inside her. Shit, the minute she hit high school, I would've taken her. That's why I have to keep her at arm's length. If we get too close, nothing is stopping us. We can't cross that line.

I pull out my phone for a distraction, noticing a few missed calls from Rachel, my latest hookup. She's been spending most of her weekends in my bed. We partnered up for a business ethics project and hit it off from there. She's not looking for a commitment, only fun. The perfect woman in my eyes.

The ride to my place is short, and Jasper's cab is leaving when we pull up. The parking lot is covered with snow and ice. We get it like a motherfucker around here. That's why I like having my truck.

"The chance I will bust my ass on the way inside is high," Nautica mutters, looking out the window. "Heels, alcohol, and ice aren't a safe combo."

"Do you want me to carry you?" I offer without thinking.

I ignore the driver's irritation at us still being in the car. She bites into her lower lip and nods. A sharp draft hits my back when I open the door and get out.

I lean down and gesture for her to move. "Come on then."

She slides to the edge of the seat and stops in front of me. I carefully bend down to pull her into my arms and lift her up. Her chilly arms clasp around my neck as she settles her face into my chest while I head toward the apartment.

"Still think this dress was a good idea?" I ask when she shivers in my arms. My mouth waters when the poor excuse of clothing rises to show me a better view of her thighs. I can feel my dick pressing against my jeans.

Fuck, she's teasing the shit out of me.

Think about something other than getting her naked.

Bunny rabbits. Football.

Shit.

Not working.

Her grip on me tightens. "It's my favorite," she says, pulling back and looking up at me with a smile.

Jasper opens the door to let us in. "I'm hitting the sheets," he calls out as I drop Nautica to her feet. He opens up the hallway closet and pulls out a blanket. "George, the couch is all yours. Good night, assholes *and* Nautica."

She's the only one who returns the good night.

She stands in the hallway, shuffling her feet while looking around nervously. My pulse springs. Now comes the time to figure out our sleeping arrangements. There's no way in hell Simon will hear about anything that happens tonight.

"Do you have something I can sleep in?" she asks, breaking the silence.

"Come on," I say, gesturing toward my bedroom.

I follow her and turn around to look at the door when we make it inside, uncertain on whether to close it. She spins around at the sound of it clicking shut. Nautica or no Nautica, I never sleep with my door open. I like my privacy.

She heads straight to my dresser and starts going through a drawer.

"Do you mind?" I ask.

She shrugs but doesn't stop. "I told you I needed something to sleep in." She whips around with a pack of condoms hanging from her fingers. "Wouldn't these be of better use in your nightstand? You know, considering that's where you do your business?"

I arch a brow and chuckle. "My bed isn't the only place I fuck, babe. You need to broaden your horizons."

She shouldn't be fucking guys, period. But I'm not an idiot. I know she went wild as soon as Simon left for the military. I tried to tell him that being so strict on her in high school would only cause her to act out more when she finally got some freedom, but he wouldn't listen to me.

"Horizons?" She snorts. "I didn't get to do shit considering you and my brother scared away all the guys who could've helped me *broaden those horizons.*"

"We did you a favor, but it's not like you're not trying to make up for it now." I clench my teeth, thinking about another guy putting his hands on her. I move forward to drag her away from the dresser. "Sit your ass down. I'll get you something," I say, pointing at my bed. I snag a pair of sweatpants and an old high school T-shirt and hand them to her.

"Thanks for letting me have your bed tonight," she says with a smirk, smacking her palm across the mattress.

"Wrong. I said you could have *the floor*."

"Come on. We both know you're not making me sleep on the floor. You're not *that* big of an asshole."

She's right.

"Fine, the bed is all yours. You know I just enjoy fucking with you."

"That's the truth," she grumbles. She bends down to take off her shoes but struggles with the clasp, almost falling off the bed.

I can't hold back my laugh. "You need some help with that?"

"Yes," she says with a sigh. "I'd appreciate it if you didn't make fun of me while doing it."

She pulls at her shoe again, and I hurry over before she face-plants on the carpet.

"The things you make me do, woman." I fall to my knees in front of her.

Her breathing hitches when I grab her foot, wrap my hand around her ankle, and unclasp the strap. The air goes thin as I pull the shoe off and toss it onto the floor. I grab her other foot and do the same.

"Thanks," she mutters when I get back to my feet.

I snag a pillow from the bed and throw it down onto the floor. The mood in the room is shifting. I can feel it. I need to separate myself before we do something stupid.

"Now, sleep off your buzz," I say.

She ignores me and leans down to pick up my pillow. My mouth falls open when she tosses it back on the bed.

"You're not sleeping on the damn floor, Bracken," she says. "We'll share the bed."

"The hell we will. Not happening." I attempt to move around her to grab my pillow back, but she blocks me.

"Shut up. We're two adults. Why are you so freaked out about it? It's not like we're going to fuck or anything."

The way she says *fuck* excites my cock.

I raise a brow. "You sure about that?"

The words slip from my lips before I have the chance to stop them. Alcohol is spiraling through my blood, and my attraction to her grows. The girl who's been off-limits to me for years is inviting me into her bed ... well, *my* bed.

She's offering her pussy to me. All I have to do now is make the first move.

She opens her mouth, hesitates, and slams it back shut. "I mean ..." She glances from side to side—waiting for me to tell her I'm only fucking around.

I take a step closer, stopping dead in front of her. "Is that what you want to happen tonight?"

Her breathing shudders, growing unsteady, and her eyes grow wild with lust.

"Do you want me to slip that tight little dress off your sexy as fuck body, lay you down on my bed, and give it to you?"

She whimpers when I snake my hand down and rub it along her thigh.

"You've been teasing me for years. Do you think it's time I finally cave and give you this cock?"

Say yes. Say yes. Please fucking say yes.

If she says no, I'll take a step back, grab my pillow, and crash on the floor.

"You know that's exactly what I want," she answers.

Those words are my undoing. The cord of restraint, discipline, restriction, everything I've been fighting with over the years has broken.

When I jerk her up from the bed, her eyes widen. I feel her breath against mine as I pull her into me and run my thumb between her lips, *back and forth*. The moment our lips meet, I know I will thoroughly enjoy this forbidden fuck. She tastes like the sugary sweet shots Jasper fed her all night.

Our kiss is carnal and urgent. Our mouths open, and I teasingly stroke my tongue against hers. Wrapping my arms around her, I guide her to the bed, and her ass bounces off the mattress when she falls back. My heart thumps like a piston while I drink her in—this woman I want on my bed waiting for me.

This is happening.

We're crossing this line.

One time.

We'll cross it only this time.

Then act like it never happened.

"You sure about this?" I'm giving her ... *us* a chance to back out.

She nods. "Positive."

When she rubs her thighs together, her dress inches up higher. My mouth falls open, taking in the sight of black lace panties covering her pussy.

Damn, she's killing me.

"Have you done this before?" I ask.

Will it stop me if she hasn't? Probably not.

I'd love to be the first man to slide inside her ... the *only* man to be inside her. I'm asking in case I need to be careful. I've only fucked two virgins, and it took them both time to adjust to my size.

She nods again. "I have."

Her response shouldn't piss me off, but it does. It's wrong for me to assume she'd wait for *us* to happen. Hell, she'd practically begged me to fuck her that night in my truck, and I shot her down. That night, I ended up screwing a random chick in the back seat while fantasizing that it was her.

It was fucked up, I know.

In my defense, it was better than actually fucking her.

Morally, at least.

Definitely not physically.

Nothing will be more satisfying than this.

She waits for my reaction, and I crawl across the bed to her. With my lips going straight to her neck, I rain kisses along her soft skin. To give me better access, she tilts her head to the side, and I suck hard.

"I want this off," I order, tugging on her dress.

When she rises to her knees and pulls her dress over her head, I lick my lips. Lust taps into my veins as I take in the beautiful sight of her wearing only her panties and bra. There's no stopping myself from cupping my balls through my jeans. She unsnaps her bra, and those full tits of hers spill out. When she goes for her panties, I grip her wrists, stopping her.

"These are mine to take off," I say. "I can't wait to fuck you."

Our lips meet again—this time more demanding, as if I own her. She bites into my lower lip as my hand lingers between her legs. My fingertips tingle as I rub her pussy through the thin material. I can't hold back any longer. I need to be inside her before I bust in my jeans, ruining the moment before it even starts.

Her back falls against the bed, and her moans echo through my room when I slip a thick finger inside her. She's already fucking soaked. I'm positive she's dripping on my sheets, which only excites me more. She's ready for me.

I slide in another finger and lean back to inspect her stretched out on my bed. Her mouthwatering tits bounce with every plunge of my fingers, and her hard nipples are begging for attention. She moans as I clamp my lips around one, sucking hard.

Her hand latches onto my hair. "Stop teasing me," she begs.

My thumb rubs her soft clit. "Teasing is the best part," I say, releasing a nipple. "Don't take away my fun." My lips go to the other nipple, sucking on it harder than the other, and I nip it with my teeth. "Plan for me to tease you here." I lick the tiny pebble and slide down the bed until my face is in line with her pussy. "And here."

Knotting my fingers around the string of her panties, I tear them down her legs. My mouth is between her legs before she even gets out another breath. I spread her wide open and curl my tongue around her clit, making slow circles. Her hand flies down to my hair and pulls it, practically ripping it from the root while she cries out.

She begs for more.

Begs for me to stop.

Begs for more.

I slip the length of my tongue inside her. She tastes delicious—so damn good. I don't slow my pace, lapping her up until she comes undone. Her body goes limp as she cries out her release.

I'm wiping my lips when I realize I'm still dressed. "I can't wait to fuck you," I whisper. I pull my shirt over my head. My jeans are next. I've never gotten undressed so damn quick in my life.

"Jesus, do you have those things stashed everywhere?" she asks when I open my nightstand and pull out a condom.

"I like being prepared." Ripping open the wrapper with my teeth, I roll the condom down my erection—dying to fill her with my cock. "You ready?"

She nods, a whimper escaping her.

"We shouldn't be doing this." My statement doesn't stop me from sliding inside her.

"I know." Her legs spread wider as she arches her back. "But nobody has to know."

My fingernails sink into the skin of her thighs as I slam into her roughly.

Fuck. This feels amazing.

"Our little secret," I grunt.

She is so fucking tight. The tightest pussy I've ever had.

I throw my head back and shut my eyes, taking in the sound of our moans.

This is the best sex I've ever had.

The best lay I've ever given.

I'll worry about the consequences later.

three

NAUTICA

"YOU WHAT?" Macy shrieks, jumping from her bed to mine after I confess I had sex with Bracken last night. "You can't be pissed off at me now. You should thank me, buy me a drink, write one of my papers next semester."

I'm back in my dorm room. My body is sore as hell, and I need rest. I kicked her bedmate out twenty minutes ago, and as soon as I collapsed on my bed, she knew something was up.

I narrow my eyes at her. "I should thank you for ditching me? If it weren't for you and your cock addiction, we wouldn't even be having this conversation right now. I wouldn't be scared out of my mind to face Bracken over break." I shake my head in annoyance. "All I can think about is him naked and inside me."

My skin flushes as images of last night sweep through my mind. I gulp, remembering his lean, sweaty body moving above me as I squirmed underneath him, begging for more. It was the hottest thing I've ever experienced, and as terrified as I am to admit it, I want to do it again.

Now that I've had a bite, I want the entire cake.

"That's a hot fucking mental image," she says with a sigh.

"And yes, you should thank me. I gave you the opportunity to screw the guy you've been panting over for years."

She pulls her blond shoulder-length hair into a loose pony-tail as she crosses her legs, eagerly waiting for me to give her details. I notice a glimpse of the early stages of a hickey breaking out along her pale skin.

"I haven't been panting over him for years," I argue.

She snorts. Macy is fully aware of my Bracken crush. "Riii-iggght. Let's not waste our time denying you've wanted to have a piece of his cock forever. Now, give me the scoop."

Making myself comfortable, I divulge last night's details: how I woke up in Bracken's bed this morning and nearly had an anxiety attack. I held my breath, fighting to stay calm, and pinched myself to be sure I wasn't dreaming.

I was scared to make a noise. I didn't want to wake him and see the look of regret in his eyes. His muscular arm was draped across my stomach like a shield, and I carefully slipped out of his hold without him stirring. I grabbed the clothes he gave me, snagged my phone and purse on the way out the door, and called a cab. I banged on the dorm door for ten minutes before Macy answered.

I climb across my bed and open the mini-fridge. "It should've never happened," I mutter. I snag a bottle of water and reach into my bag for ibuprofen. I have a headache, a hang-over from hell, and regret is my middle name.

"Oh please, you two have been beating around the *fuck me* bush for years now. I mean, the guy stops what he's doing whenever you call him. He likes you. He may be too pussy to admit it, but he does." She bounces off my bed and gets back into hers. "And FYI, I'm totally jealous. I wish you hadn't called dibs on him first."

That's one thing Macy has never done. She's never tried to

sleep with Bracken because she knows my feelings for him. He's the only guy I've ever crushed on.

"Simon is going to freak out." My stomach churns at the thought of what his reaction will be. He'll be pissed, and I'm not sure if he'll ever forgive Bracken ... or me for causing him to lose his best friend.

"That's why you're not telling him. You're going to keep your mouth shut, and so is Bracken."

"But what if he finds out? He'll be angrier over us hiding it from him."

"God, your brother doesn't have to know every single damn detail of your life, Nautica. You're an adult. It's not like Bracken took your virginity."

"What if Bracken feels guilty and tells him?"

A long breath runs from her lips. "He's not that fucking stupid. He won't risk your brother hating him. You two giving each other the business one drunken night is a story that'll never be told again. Keep your mouth shut. He won't say anything. I won't say anything. All will be good in the world."

"I hope you're right."

"I'm always right." She grabs her eye mask and pulls it over her head. "Now, let's get some sleep. I'm sore as hell and feel like shit."

I make myself comfortable and close my eyes, but sleep doesn't come to me. What does, though, is my imagination running wild. All I can think about is how amazing Bracken's hands felt against my skin and how skilled he was with his tongue.

When I finally get to sleep, I dream about last night happening again.

Houston, we have a problem.

four
BRACKEN

"OFF-LIMITS, HUH?" Jasper asks when I walk into the kitchen, barefoot and sleepy-eyed. A shit-eating grin is on his face as he snags a box of cereal. "I didn't know you were exempt from that rule."

"I don't know what the fuck you're talking about," I reply, sitting down at the table.

My head is blasting against my skull with fear. I'm going to lose my best friend—all because I couldn't keep my dick in my pants and out of his little sister.

I heard Nautica sneaking out this morning but faked sleep, which makes me a fucking coward. I couldn't face her. I wanted to beg her to stay. We needed to talk about it, but I didn't know what to say. I was too chickenshit. I fucked up, and I fucked up bad.

Ten minutes after she left, I pulled myself out of bed and noticed she forgot her dress during her walk of shame.

I slept with my best friend's little sister. In my defense, she's not so little anymore. She's grown. The way she rode my cock last night and moaned my name further proves my argument.

Simon is going to kick my ass when he finds out. He's trusted me around her for years, and I betrayed him.

Sure, we'd been drinking, but I can't get away with that excuse. I wasn't that drunk, and she looked so damn sexy. Whenever I saw another guy eye-fucking her, the harder I craved to touch her. When she was in my bedroom, it hit me. There was no more denying myself the person I've wanted for years.

"I don't know what I'm talking about?" Jasper asks mockingly. "Your headboard was banging against the wall like we were having an earthquake. There's no mistaking what was going on in there." He groans. "The moans, fuck, man, the moans. They were so hot. I was tempted to jack off."

I rub my hands over my face. "It shouldn't have happened. We were both drunk … one thing led to another … and …"

"And the next thing you knew, you were balls deep in her sweet little pussy?" He pours milk over his cereal. "You better hope her brother doesn't find out about your little orgasm escapade."

If Simon finds out I slept with Nautica, he'll never speak to me again. He became the man of the house after their father died during a tour in Iraq. He was reluctant about her attending college here but agreed after I promised to watch out for her.

"Everyone needs to keep their mouths shut about last night," I say.

"You know I won't say anything, bro."

Hot pebbles of water sprinkle down my back as I wash away the rough feeling of my hangover. I tip my head down to look at my hard cock.

Nautica hasn't left my mind since she ran out of my bed. I

shut my eyes and imagine how great it would feel to have her lips around my cock, sucking me. My hand wanders down and wraps tightly around my erection. I stroke myself. My arm moves faster. I'm getting closer as I remember how good her pussy tasted. I can't stop. I groan out my release and watch my cum wash down the drain.

I'm so fucked.

I'm going home for the holidays. So is Simon—which means I'll be seeing Nautica way too fucking much to keep my hands to myself.

* * *

My stomach knots when I see Simon's name flashing across my phone screen. My lungs inhale a long breath before I answer the call.

"Hey, man."

"Hey, what's going on?" he asks.

He sounds cool and collected. No animosity detected yet.

Good sign.

I clear my throat, hoping I don't sound as guilty as I feel. "Not shit, dude. Just finished up with finals."

"You're going home for break, right?"

"Yeah. You know my dad will kick my ass if I'm not there for all the holiday shit. He wants me to look at the dealership. It's time I choose my office."

One more semester to go, and I'll be there working full-time.

He laughs. Another good sign. "Good. I need you to do me a favor."

"Sure, what's up?"

"Can you give Nautica a lift? She planned on riding home with Macy, but Macy isn't coming home until next week now."

Is this a test?

"Sure. Yeah. That's no problem."

"Thanks. I'll buy you a drink when I get home. I appreciate you watching out for her while she's been there. You have no idea how relieved I am knowing you have my back."

"Glad I can help out." *Oh, and by the way, I fucked her brains out last night. How's that for watching out for her?* "I'll see you in a few days."

"I'll give you some gas money."

"Don't worry about it. I'm already coming home. It's no big deal."

Simon offers me money every time I do something for his family, but I never accept it. I'm fortunate enough that my family can help me out and pay my tuition, but his mom doesn't have it like that.

I hang up with him and dial Nautica's number. I'm nervous as fuck to talk to her, but sending a text seems too much like a lame-ass move. She'll think I lost my balls or some shit.

Pick up.

Don't pick up.

It's one of those phone calls you fucking dread and secretly hope they won't answer so you can leave a voicemail. Then we'll play phone tag and end up texting instead. It's the way of communication these days. No talking, only words on a screen.

"Hello?" The sound of her angelic voice surprises me and causes my dick to stir.

Stop, dumbass.

I take another deep breath. *Why the fuck am I so nervous?* I'm never anxious around chicks.

"Hey, how are you doing?" My question comes out like a stutter. I fucking stutter.

"Good," she answers with a hint of shyness.

I need to cut to the chase and get the awkward part out, so we can move on. "Do you want to talk about it?"

She clears her throat. "Not particularly."

Numbness invades my chest.

Does she want to act like it never happened?

Does she regret it?

I nod even though she can't see me. "Okay, now that we have that out of the way, when do you want to head home?"

"I don't care, whenever. You're the one driving."

"Tomorrow at noon okay?"

"Sounds good." The air goes silent for a few seconds. "And thanks for the ride."

"You know you don't have to thank me for that shit." I pull my phone away from my ear when a call comes through.

Rachel.

I hit the ignore button.

"I guess ... I'll see you tomorrow."

"See you then."

My phone rings again as soon as I hang up.

Rachel.

"Hey," I answer with hesitation, hoping she doesn't want to come over.

I can't have another chick in my bed. Nautica's scent is still lingering on my sheets.

"Hey handsome, let me in," she says with a chuckle. "I've been knocking on the door for five minutes."

"Fuck, I didn't hear you."

I'd been so wrapped up in Nautica I wasn't paying attention to anything else. I stagger out of my bedroom and head to the door.

She's shaking snowflakes out of her fire-red hair when I open it, wearing a bright smile on her face. "Sorry for showing up out of the blue. I got off work and thought I'd pay you a visit before we leave for break."

I follow her down the hallway and into my bedroom. She takes off her coat and unwraps the scarf around her neck. She sheds her shirt next, giving me a full view of the delicious tits spilling out of a bra that matches her hair.

"I'm also horny as hell and in desperate need of a good lay," she adds. "You weren't answering my calls last night." Her wind-burned lips form a frown.

She reaches for my hand and guides me to the bed. I rub the back of my neck and try to look away when she straddles my lap.

Fuck! I should've kept her ass in the living room. I knew this shit was going to happen. Rachel only comes over when she wants to fuck.

"I knew you were the best person for the job." She rocks her hips against me.

I suck in a breath, begging my cock not to get excited, but it's not listening. I can feel the pressure building up between my legs as she rubs her warm pussy against me.

Can I fuck her only hours after my dick was inside Nautica?

If it were any other chick last night, I wouldn't give a shit, but it was Nautica. She's different, and I feel like a scumbag for even having Rachel in my bed.

My hands plant on her hips to stop her. "I'm actually feeling pretty tired. I was up late last night."

My lame-ass excuse doesn't work. My head tilts back as she fights against my hold, sliding back and forth against my cock again.

"You might be tired, but your cock doesn't feel the same way."

I stop her again. "I can't." The words peter out of my mouth.

Her green eyes study me as she leans back. "Since when do you turn down sex?"

"I fucked someone last night."

My confession seems to shock us both.

"I doubt you'd be too happy getting sloppy seconds," I add.

She slides off my lap and starts dressing. "Thank you for being honest. I don't know if I should be pissed or grateful. She must be pretty special if you're turning down sex for her. Let me know if anything changes."

I don't bother chasing after her when she walks out of my room.

five

NAUTICA

"WHEN IS SIMON PICKING YOU UP?" Macy asks, zipping up her suitcase.

Simon is coming home for the holidays, which is exciting to both my mom and me. I was only able to talk to him on the phone a few times while he's been away at basic training.

"He's not."

She turns around and looks at me with confusion.

"Bracken is giving me a ride."

My plan had been to ride home with Macy, but she decided to spend the first week of break in Florida with her mom. Her parents had given her the gift of divorce for her graduation present. Apparently, they'd wanted it for years but agreed to wait until after she finished high school to split up. They couldn't hold back any longer and broke the news to her that night. Her mom's bags were already packed and sitting by the front door. I spent that night by her side, taking turns drinking out of a cheap bottle of vodka and holding back her hair as she puked it up later.

"Bracken is giving you a ride?" she asks. "Bracken, as in the off-limits best friend of your brother that you bumped uglies with a few nights ago?"

I set a stack of folded clothes in my suitcase. "Bracken isn't a very popular name," I reply sarcastically, resulting in a pillow to my face.

"Are you going to give him a ride in the back seat of that sexy as fuck truck?"

"Really, Macy? You just said he was off-limits to me."

She snorts. "Just because you're not *supposed* to do it doesn't mean you can't indulge a little bit, break some rules. Let him eat your pussy or something."

I rub my thighs together, remembering how amazing his tongue felt between my legs and against my warmth. The man knows how to use his tongue.

"Have you heard from him?" Her question breaks me away from my thoughts.

"He called yesterday."

"And?"

"He asked how I was doing and if I wanted to talk about it. Obviously, I said no. Then he asked when I wanted to head home." I shrug. "That's about it."

She frowns. "You do know you two have to talk about it sooner or later? He's too close with your family to avoid it. You keep delaying the inevitable, and it will only get worse. Shit might blow up in your faces. You have a six-hour car ride home, so do it then." She smacks my side, her frown morphing into a grin. "And if you get some dick after it, good for you, girl. You deserve a nice little Christmas present."

six

BRACKEN

"BE CAREFUL, BE VERY CAREFUL," Jasper sings out. He slaps me on the back while I lock my bedroom door from the outside. He's never fucked with my shit, but I don't want any of his company to think my bed has an open vacancy.

"Don't do anything I wouldn't do," he goes on and pauses for a moment before giving me a sly smile. "Actually, I'd probably fuck her again, so scratch that last statement. I'd never use me as a reference in that saying because there's not much shit I wouldn't do when it comes to getting some pussy."

"I'm well aware of that," I mumble, heading toward the kitchen. I grab my mini-cooler from the pantry and start packing it with ice. "How about you not try to get your brain bashed in while I'm gone? I can't afford rent here by myself, and it's hell trying to find a new roommate in the middle of the year."

He scratches his head and joins me in the kitchen. "Why'd you think that'd happen?"

I pull out bottles of water from the fridge and pack them in the cooler. My dad taught me to always be prepared. "By sticking your cock into the pussy of another guy's girlfriend."

"Oh yeah, sorry about that." He's still smiling, not even fazed by the wake-up call we received this morning from some asshole screaming on our doorstep, adamant about kicking Jasper's ass. "It's not like she told me she had a boyfriend."

"Next time, start asking. He had forty pounds on you."

Jasper isn't scrawny, but he also isn't built. He's tall and lean. I had to jump in and stop the guy from smashing his head in with a baseball bat.

"Make smarter decisions. I'll see you in a few weeks."

"You do the same. Keep your dick in your pants around any chicks named Nautica," he yells as I walk out the door.

A new kick of memories shoots through my mind every time she's brought up. My cock instantly remembers how good she felt. My brain might be screaming that it's not smart thinking about her like that, but my dick isn't in agreement.

I throw my bag and the cooler into the back seat and head toward campus. It's snowing hard, so I keep my speed down. Even though my truck does well in shitty weather, I still have to be careful.

I was infatuated with trucks before I could even drive. My grandpa had one. My dad has one. Growing up, I knew it was the only thing I wanted to drive. I worked for my dad during my summer breaks in high school, saved up money, and bought my first truck from him when I turned sixteen. My parents surprised me with a brand new one on my graduation day. I'm now in my senior year of college working on my business degree so I can take over my dad's car dealerships when he retires.

I send Nautica a text telling her I'm on my way. My apartment is a few miles away from campus housing. I prefer not to deal with the undergrad drunken bullshit. I spent my freshman year in the dorms, and it was hell. I didn't have the patience to deal with disorderly drunken idiots, nor did I have a problem with telling them that. After getting into three fights with my roommate, I knew I wasn't going through another year of it, and my parents let me move into my apartment.

I pull into the first open parking spot and take the stairs up to Nautica's floor. I've only been in her dorm once when I helped her mom move her in because Simon was gone. I usually drop her off at the entrance when she stays over.

I ignore the smiles and whistles shooting my way as I head down the all-girls hallway. Her door flies open after my first knock. Macy is standing in front of me wearing a pair of tiny-ass shorts and a tank top, sans bra. Her nipples are hard, and her lips form a smile when she sees me. I already know she's going to be a pain in my ass.

"Bracken." She says my name with a purr and a bite of her lower lip. "To what do I owe the pleasure?" She rests her hands on her slim hips and kicks her right leg out.

There's no denying that Macy is attractive, but she's not my type. It's not that I don't like her or the fact that she explores her sexuality. Shit, I've probably fucked more people than she has. What pisses me off about her is that she's a shitty-ass friend to Nautica. She's constantly ditching her and has for years. Not to mention, she drags her to damn near every party on campus.

"Nautica," I respond.

Macy is still on my shit list for leaving Nautica at the bar. I should probably be thanking her for allowing me to get the best pussy of my life, but I don't.

She gives me a sideways look. "She already left."

I take a step back. "Wait, what?"

Did she find another ride home?

There's no way she'd do that without telling me, right?

"Macy, stop messing with him," Nautica calls out, appearing at her friend's side. She opens up the door wider, grabbing Macy's arm so I can slide into the room. "Let me grab my bag, and I'll be ready to go."

I nod. Her room looks the same as when I helped her unpack. Her side is organized perfectly, which doesn't surprise me. Her bed is made, a yellow comforter spread across the twin mattress, and fuzzy pillows are lined up near the head of it. She's been a neat freak for as long as I can remember.

She says goodbye to Macy. I don't. I grab her bag, and she follows me out to my truck. I crank up the heat as soon as we get in, then reach into the back seat to open the cooler and snag her a water.

"You ready for this long drive?" I ask, backing out of the parking spot.

It's a six-hour drive from here to Colorado.

She groans and signals out the window. "It would be better if the weather wasn't so shitty. I only like snow on Christmas."

"We live in Colorado. How are you not used to this weather yet?"

"I'm used to it, but that doesn't mean I like it."

I nod. "How does it feel to have your first semester of college over with?"

"Relieving," she says, twisting the bottle cap open. "I mean, you hear rumors about finals being hell week, but it's actually true. Luckily, I did pretty well, but I lost count of the number of hours I spent studying."

"Do you think you did okay?"

She nods. "Yep. What about you? Are you ready to be done with it all and work for your dad? A lot of people don't work well with their family."

"I look up to my dad, enjoy hanging out with him, and can't wait to show him what I'm made of."

My dad has some flaws, but we all do. He's a good father

and an even better businessman. I can't wait to have his role when I take over his multiple car dealerships.

"I'm sure you'll do well. You're a sweet talker."

"Oh, really?"

"Yes, really. All you have to do is give that charming smile and say a few words to a woman, and she'll buy a car from you. Shit, she'll buy anything from you. You're a smooth talker."

"Does that work with you, too? Will you do anything I ask?" I slam my mouth shut. I shouldn't have asked that.

She eyes the floor. "Obviously, look what happened the other night."

I open my mouth to answer, to fix this, but my phone ringing stops me.

Saved by the damn ringtone.

"It's your dad," she tells me, grabbing it from the cup holder.

"Answer it for me."

The weather is getting worse. My hands aren't leaving the steering wheel.

"Hi Randy, it's Nautica," she answers casually. "I'm going to put you on speaker."

She's tight with my family. My parents love her.

She holds the phone up in the air as my dad's voice shoots through my truck.

"The roads are getting worse, and it looks like the storm is headed straight in your direction. If they get too bad, you need to stop. Rent a hotel room and wait until it clears up. You don't need to be driving in this weather," he says.

"Got it," I answer. "We'll be careful and keep in touch."

Nautica talks to him for a few minutes about her finals before hanging up. Our sex conversation isn't brought back up, and we spend the next two hours listening to the weather channel. My speed decreases with every mile as the roads grow slicker. The man on the radio confirms that a blizzard is headed our way.

Just perfect.

When we get to the interstate, it's an even bigger mess. Every car is moving slow with their emergency lights on, so the car behind them can see where they're going. I keep my eyes on the road, scared of hitting black ice. I'm not even sure if we're staying in our lane. I grip the steering wheel so tight I'm surprised it doesn't break in fear that we'll slide.

"I think we need to stop," I tell her. "It's getting too bad. I don't want to risk it."

"I agree," she says. "It looks like there's an exit coming up in a few miles. I'm sure there will be somewhere we can wait until the storm blows over."

* * *

"One or two rooms?" the guy behind the hotel's front desk asks.

His eyes transfer between Nautica and me curiously, which pisses me off. I'm sure we aren't the first two people of the opposite sex to come in looking for a place to crash. I want to punch him in his crooked smile for the way he's staring at Nautica.

I look over at her in question. I never thought about getting separate rooms.

"One room. Two beds," I answer him but keep my eyes on her. "We're only going to be here until the storm calms and the roads clear. It's stupid to pay for two rooms."

And the thought of hanging out in a hotel room alone for hours sounds like a fucking bore. I need some damn company.

She nods in agreement. "One room it is. *Two beds.*"

I hand the guy my credit card while she sifts through her

massive-sized purse. "Here, I'll pay half," she offers, pulling out her wallet.

That isn't fucking happening.

I hold up my hand to stop her, resulting in a frown coming my way. "Don't worry about it."

She's just as bad as her brother is about accepting handouts.

"I'd have to pay for a room whether you were here or not."

She tucks her wallet back in her bag at the same time the guy hands me our key card.

"You're in room two twelve," he tells us.

I grab Nautica's bag, along with mine, and follow her toward the elevator. I set our bags down on each bed when we make it into the room and take a look around.

Two full beds, a bathroom, a mini-fridge, and a TV. Not a dump but nothing special. It's a standard room. There weren't many hotel choices on the exit we took, so we settled for the nicest one we could find.

"Might as well make ourselves comfortable," I say, shrugging off my coat as she does the same.

I snag the remote from the nightstand and collapse onto the bed. I keep my eyes on her as she slowly progresses across the room to the other bed. There were so many times I wanted to continue our conversation about our night together, but I kept my mouth shut in fear she didn't want it brought up.

What is going through her mind about me?

About us?

Is she going to tell Simon?

"I guess so," she replies, hesitation sliding along her words.

This wouldn't be so awkward if I hadn't fucked her the other night. We would be joking around and comfortable around each other. Things are different now. I should've thought with my brain instead of my cock.

She slides off her shoes and makes herself comfortable on the bed. I look around, suddenly becoming aware of the situation we're in, realizing I set myself up for disaster. We're so close and in a hotel room *alone*.

All I can think about is the multitude of dirty things I can do to her on that bed. How I can slowly undress and kiss every inch of her delicious body and fuck her again like I've been fantasizing about nonstop. I can stand up, take one step, and touch her.

I should be fighting, resisting these urges, but I'm only feeding them with my imagination. Thoughts of how amazing it would feel to pass the time between her legs and how badly I want to feel her suck my cock won't leave me.

I shake my head. I need to pull myself together. Leaning back against the headboard, I try to concentrate on the weatherman. Fuck, more snow, and it doesn't look like it's stopping anytime soon. We're going to be here for a while.

I'm going to be locked in a room with my temptation and no way to escape for who knows how long. This is going to be a motherfucker.

"Now that we know we're stuck here, let's watch something decent," she says.

"Sounds good. What are you up for? We can rent a movie?" I suggest, tossing the remote over to her. "You pick."

She flips through the movies and stops on the one I definitely don't want to watch.

"Nuh-uh, anything but that. I'm not up for watching dudes strip down to that 'Ride My Pony' song. I'd rather watch the damn weatherman."

Shit, I'd rather watch Dr. fucking Phil.

"Hey, I love *Magic Mike*," she whines, pouting out her lip. "I haven't had a chance to see the new one."

"That's great. Love it when I'm not with you."

She gives me a dirty look. "Really? So much for you letting me pick. What do you want to watch then? Guys with guns shooting up shit and jumping off buildings?"

"That actually sounds much better."

We go back and forth over potential movie options before I cave and let her watch the damn male stripper movie.

There's no saying no to her.

seven

NAUTICA

I STRUGGLE to get comfortable as I try to keep my focus on the TV, but I can't stop thinking about the man stretched out on the bed beside mine. Even with the sexy men ripping off their clothes and dry humping the air on the screen, my mind is on him.

He wins.

Bracken Casey will always win my heart, but all I'll ever get from him is a one-night stand.

Not even a consolation prize.

My heart putters like a drum, smashing into my rib cage like a wrecking ball filled with nervousness. I'm using every ounce of self-restraint I have not to jump on his bed and attack him.

I take a few breaths and relax against my pillow as flickers of our night together come to mind. I acted drunker than I really was. In the back of my mind, I had a plan—blame it on the alcohol if he rejected me. The next morning, I'd act like I had no recollection of the events that had taken place. The problem is that I hadn't expected him to actually kiss me. I definitely didn't expect him to have sex with me. That entire night was filled with new experiences that I thought would never happen.

One more time.

Maybe we can do it just *one* more time. It will be a way for us to fight our boredom and will cure my craving. One more time, and maybe I can get him out of my system. One more time, and maybe he'll realize what he's been missing all along —what's been right in front of him for years.

"I hate to burst your bubble, babe, but this movie is fucking ridiculous," he says, breaking me away from my thoughts. "I can't believe people actually pay to watch this shit. It's horrible."

I turn on my side to look at him. "You know how some people watch porn?"

He arches a brow, uncertain of where I'm going with this.

I roll my eyes. "Don't try to act like you don't watch porn."

His arm swings out to gesture toward the TV. "What the fuck does me watching porn have to do with this shit? There's no tits, no ass, no penetration. Nothing entertaining."

"It's like PG-13 porn."

He snorts at my response.

"Hey, not all of us want to see *tits, ass, and penetration.* We only want a little eye candy."

A salacious grin breaks out along his lips. "Have you ever even watched porn before, Nautica?" His voice is husky—his tone full of challenge.

The room grows warm as my heart pounds against my chest.

"That's none of your business." I fake being more annoyed than I actually am.

"So you haven't?"

I want to smack away the humiliating blush rising along my cheekbones. "Again, that's none of your business."

He wiggles his finger my way. "Give me the remote."

I arch a brow. "Why?"

"Give. Me. The. Remote."

My hand wavers before I toss it to him. I stare at the TV while he turns off the movie and starts flipping through the pay-per-view options. My mouth falls open, but no words form when I realize what he's doing.

No way.

I'm going to kill him.

He's only fucking with me.

He won't go there.

Will he?

My legs tingle. I want to dash out of this room, flee with embarrassment, and lock myself in his truck. But I can't move. I'm frozen in place. Curiosity is a motherfucker digging at my mind and convincing me to stay.

Excitement grows in the pit of my belly. I stay silent while he scrolls through the *Adult Videos XXX* list.

College Coeds Untamed.

Bessie's Back Door Experience.

Lola's Lost Innocence.

Where the hell do they even come up with these names?

"Bracken?" I say slowly—surprised words can even leave my mouth. "What are you doing?"

He shrugs without bothering to look at me. "Giving you your first true porn experience. I want to show you it's more exciting and enlightening than your PG-13, boring shit."

I scrape a hand through my hair and bite into my lip. "What?" I suck in a breath. "What if I don't want any porn experience? What if I want to stay a porn virgin for life?"

Shit! I just admitted I haven't watched it before.

"That sucks for you and whatever chump you marry."

I frown and am in too much shock of him insulting my future husband to realize he's selected a movie until I see the word *loading* on the screen. I slam my eyes shut, refusing to watch, and then cup my hands over my ears, refusing to listen.

My hands are failing because I hear the slow, instrumental music playing, but I don't hear any moans or groans ... yet.

"Move your hands away and open your damn eyes, Nautica," he says, his tone demanding.

I squeeze my eyes tighter and shake my head.

He lets out a ragged breath of annoyance. "Fine, shit. Do you want me to turn it off?"

I loosen my hands. I can hear voices. A man's ... then a woman's. She calls him professor.

Role-playing.

Teacher and student, I assume.

I shake my head again, not saying anything. I don't want him to turn it off, but I also don't want to admit how turned on I'm getting.

"Your dad," I croak out. "He's ... he's going to see this on the bill."

And think what the fuck?

I can only imagine what his parents would think of me if they knew I was peeping porn with their son.

"He isn't going to see shit. I paid for the room with my credit card. No one will know about this but you and me. It'll be our little secret."

Another one to add to the list.

We're starting to rack up quite a collection of those.

I pry open one eye, then the other, and take a deep breath before staring at the TV. I don't look at Bracken. I don't have the guts to, but I can feel his eyes on me, anticipating my reaction.

There's a woman, probably in her early twenties, blond, busty, and gorgeous. She's sitting on a desk with her legs spread open, giving us a view of her goods. A man stands in front of her, rubbing his hand up and down her legs while sporting a wild grin.

My mouth falls open when his hand moves underneath her skirt. He starts stroking her between the legs. Her curls hit the desk as her head falls back, and she cries out in ecstasy. Her eyes slam shut, and she moves in sync with his fingers. The moans come next. They're loud, high-pitched, and overexaggerated.

Is that how I look when I'm horny and on the brink of an orgasm?

God, I hope not.

I block out the moans and pick up on Bracken's sharp breaths. He's turned on. I gulp, going back and forth with myself on whether to look at him.

The girl drops to her knees, her mouth opening as she takes in his gigantic cock. He looks down, watching her intently, and grips her hair while telling her what a good student she is.

My breathing grows ragged as heat explodes through me. I fight with myself, dying to inch my fingers underneath my panties and put out the fire building between my thighs.

It's hot. It's intense. It's dirty.

Porn isn't so bad after all.

It's actually pretty fucking amazing.

Bracken might've introduced a new drug to an addict.

The guy flips the woman over, smashing his front against her back, and slides inside her from behind. Their moans, grunts, and the sound of their smacking flesh takes over the silence of us. Our heavy breathing and loud sighs are our only signs of communication.

Bracken clears his throat when the movie ends, and his voice is barely a whisper, "So?"

I stay quiet, certain if I talk, it won't be pretty. I'm either going to scream at him or try to seduce him.

Possibly both.

He clears his throat again. "What did you think?"

"I think I'm pissed at you," I say, finally gaining the guts to look at him.

His hands are clenched to his sides, his front teeth biting into his lower lip, and I can make out the length of his excitement under his jeans.

"I'm pissed at you because you made me watch that. Now I'm horny as hell with no way to relieve myself."

"Fix it then." His eyes blaze into mine.

I shake my head, gaping at him like he's a madman. "There's no way I'm masturbating in front of you."

"Do you want me to fix it for you?"

My mouth falls open. My breathing restricts as I pinch myself, certain I'm clouded in a dream. But I'm not dreaming. I'm here … with Bracken … and he's waiting on my response to whether I want him to finger fuck me or not.

"Now is not the time to mess with me." The throbbing between my legs is torturous. I don't have time for his jesting. He needs to shut me down, so I can attempt to calm myself.

I wait for his smart-ass response, for him to break out in laughter, but that's not what I get. His eyes are determined, his face stolid. He points at his erection, his teeth gritting in the process.

"Do you see this?" he asks. "Do you see how fucking hard my dick is? Do you think I'm bullshitting with you?"

I blink a few times before meeting his eyes.

"I repeat, do you want me to fix it for you? Say the word, and it's fucking done."

The air in the room grows thick. I'm screaming on the inside, bursting at the seams with excitement, but I keep my voice calm. I want to sound seductive and sexy, like the girl in the video.

"Yes, Bracken. I do. I want you to come to my bed, strip off my clothes, shove your fingers inside me, and make me come like he did to that girl."

Holy shit, did I really just say that?

Did those words actually fall from my lips?

I'm blaming it on post-porn watching side effects.

They need a warning label on that shit. *"If you watch this, you'll try to screw your brother's best friend ... or really anyone."*

I stay still as he leans forward. The tip of his finger hits the remote, and the TV goes black. He slithers out of bed without saying a word. His strong jaw flexes, and he squares up his shoulders. The look of uncertainty morphs into something that resembles determination.

There's no turning back now. He doesn't have a damn problem with it.

That makes two of us.

He stops at the side of my bed. "I have an idea."

"What's that?"

He sheds his T-shirt, and I can't stop myself from feathering my fingers across the sculpted muscles of his chest. He looks down at my hand and pumps up his hips. "Let's play a game to see who can get the other off first."

I raise a brow. "I'm always up for a challenge."

I run my hand over his hard bulge. His back straightens when I unzip his jeans and slowly slide my fingers underneath them. I roughly cup him through his boxers.

Oh yeah, he's ready for me, and I can't wait to touch him.

"Then show me what you've got." His tone is sharp as he looks down at me. He bucks his hips forward as further invitation.

Things are about to get a lot more entertaining in this podunk hotel room.

I get up on my knees and forcefully yank his pants down

along with his boxers. His throbbing erection springs forth directly in front of my face. My mouth waters, and my panties are soaked.

My tongue races across the bottom of my lip as I grab his cock with both hands. He jerks forward when I pump my hands up and down in opposite directions, feeling the full length of him growing harder.

"God, don't stop," he mutters, throwing his head back.

I don't listen to him. Instead, I replace my hands with my tongue as I circle it around his tip and lick away the small bead of pre-cum.

"Fuck, yeah. That's even better," he says, tilting up his hips. "Suck me good. Show me how you're going to win."

I'm beginning to realize why Bracken has girls falling at his feet. The man knows how to fuck, and he knows how to talk dirty while doing it.

I sweep my tongue over his length before taking him in my mouth. He's big ... larger than what I'm used to, and it takes me a second to adjust to his size.

He groans, moving up his pelvis to feed me more, and I suck harder, positive I'm going to win, but he stops me.

"Don't think I give up that easy, sweetheart," he says, grinning.

His cock falls from my mouth with a plop, and I shriek when he grabs me underneath my arms and throws me backward on the bed. "I do not like losing."

I gasp, anxiously waiting for what's coming next as he joins me in the bed.

He strips off my shirt. I wriggle out of my jeans. Our eyes meet, and we stare at each other for a minute.

"Come here," he says, falling down on his back. His eyes fasten on me as I crawl over to him. "Now, turn your ass around."

I do as I'm told and look back at him from over my shoulder.

"Feed me your pussy."

I freeze.

He smiles. "It's too late to get shy on me now." He points at his cock. "I take care of you. You take care of me. Let's see who does the better job."

I chew on the edge of my lip. I've never done this before. Sure, I've given blowjobs, and guys other than Bracken have gone down on me, but I've never done them simultaneously. My sex life didn't take off until college, so my experience is on a completely different level than his.

He bends forward to snag my leg and drags me his way. I take slow, deep breaths and carefully position myself over him. He doesn't waste any time. His tongue immediately goes between my legs. All the hesitation of not being experienced enough for him is wiped away with his first lick. I'm a goner.

"Oh, fuck," I moan, my mouth falling open directly over his erection.

I grin, dipping my head down and wrapping my lips around the tip. He jerks underneath me as I draw his entire length into my mouth. His tongue is causing me to have a hard time focusing on my own job of sucking his cock. I need to get my shit together before I lose our little game.

His powerful hand grips my ass and draws me closer to him. I pull back when he smacks my ass. He's playing dirty. He's eating my pussy for the win, and I need to suck his cock the same way.

I level myself with one hand, take him completely in my mouth, and use my other hand to massage his balls.

His tongue moves faster. I suck him harder. We're getting closer and closer.

I lose it when he shoves two fingers inside me. They move in sync with his tongue, bringing me to my brink. I don't give a shit if I win or lose at this point, I'm only worried about one thing: getting off. And that's what I do as I embarrassingly scream out my release.

Seconds later, I taste the saltiness of his cum filling my mouth. I suck him dry and swallow down every bit.

"Let's call that a tie," he says, slapping my ass again.

I blow out a long breath and pull away from him. Silence devours us. The lights flicker a few times, and the room goes dark.

"Please tell me the electricity just didn't go out," I mutter, blinking.

"I think so," he answers with a chuckle.

I groan. "Go fucking figure." At least I don't have to face him. That's a plus.

"I think it's a sign."

"A sign for what? The world is now ending because I sucked your cock?"

I shiver as his cold hand runs along the inside of my thigh. "I think it's a sign we need to cure our boredom again."

He grabs my hand, placing it over his cock, as it hardens underneath my palm. I straddle his lap and slowly take him inside me.

We fuck in the darkness of the deserted hotel room.

Our little secret.

eight

BRACKEN

"DO you want to talk about it?" I ask, buckling my seat belt.

I merge onto the interstate to go home. The streets are still in pretty rough condition, but they're plowed.

The darkness stayed as we fucked and while we groaned out our releases. It must've come on during the night because we had light this morning.

Thank fuck.

"Talk about what?" Nautica replies. Her voice is cold and distant. *Not good.* She's staring down at her phone like it's the most fascinating thing she's ever seen.

She's playing the innocent act, but I know now there's no innocence flowing through her veins. There's a wildcat under there, and the sensitive fingernail scrapes on my back further prove my point.

"About last night," I say.

We'd done it again—severed the rules. Delight shouldn't have fogged my mind when I woke up this morning with her ass plastered against my dick and my arms wrapped around her, but it did. It was so much better than feigning sleep while she snuck out. This morning was awkward. We barely said a word to each other as we brushed our teeth, changed clothes, and left.

"Nope," she answers sharply.

"You kidding me?" I have to know where her head is before we get home. We need to figure out a plan so we don't get ourselves caught up.

She releases a long, ragged breath as her eyes deadpan on me. "No, I'm not *kidding* you. If we talk about it, you're probably going to tell me it was wrong and can't happen again."

I stupidly nod in agreement.

"I don't want to hear you say those words because I don't agree with them." She signals back and forth between us. "Us together, you and me, it's not wrong. It's perfect to me, and I know you feel the same way. So excuse me if I don't want to hear you stutter out lies like, *"this can't happen again,"* when we both know damn well you want it to. Quit worrying about my brother. He'll get over it. We're grown adults."

I'm lost for words. I wasn't expecting all of that. This is worse than I thought. She wants us to be more than a hookup. She wants commitment.

I want all of Nautica, but commitment isn't my thing. I'm not looking for a girlfriend or a wife. I enjoy fucking her, but that's as far as shit will go between us.

She's eyeing me with expectancy, like her proclamation will change everything, and we'll be all hearts and roses.

"You know that can't happen," I say.

Her face shifts from hopeful to hostile.

"It was a one-time thing."

"A *one-time thing* that's happened *three times*." She holds up three fingers and lets out a harsh laugh. "That makes real sense." Her purse lands on the floorboard with a thud, and she kicks her legs up on the dashboard. "God, I'm so damn stupid."

"You're not stupid. *I'm* the dumbass for leading you on."

"Yes, I am stupid. I thought maybe, *just maybe,* you might see me as more than your best friend's little sister. Of course, I was wrong. You'll never see me like that. You only touched me because I was convenient and you were horny. I'm like all those other girls, the ones you hook up with but get freaked out when they want a commitment."

I violently shake my head. "That's not true. Don't compare yourself to those chicks. You know you're fucking different. You're so much more."

I shouldn't have brought this up. Keeping my mouth shut is the smartest thing I could've done. Now, she hates me because I can't explain to her how I feel.

"I'm different because you have to see me again. I bet you won't even tell Simon. You're too much of a coward to tell him you screwed his sister."

"You're damn straight I don't want him to know, so I'd appreciate you keeping your mouth shut. You know I'm attracted to you. You're sexy, smart, and a giant pain in my ass, but I enjoy hanging out with you. Sure, there might be something more with us, but we can't explore that. We know it won't go anywhere, and you know I don't date."

"All right then," she says with a glare. "We got each other out of our systems. Now, we can move on to bigger and better things."

I let out a growl. I'm not okay with other motherfuckers putting their hands, mouth, or cock anywhere near here. There is no *bigger or better* than me. I don't want anyone else to have her, but I can't cross that line. I'm a selfish man.

"You were right. It's not a good idea to talk about this shit," I fire back.

I turn up the volume on the radio and concentrate on the road. She pulls out a book, and the ride goes eerily quiet. It's another four hours until we make it home. Four long as hell hours.

The sound of her moaning my name is much more gratifying than her silence.

* * *

"Do you want me to help with your bag?" I offer, pulling into her driveway, not wanting us to end on bad terms.

"Nope," she snaps, her first word in hours.

I jump out of my truck, ignoring her answer, and walk around to meet her. I open the back door and capture her bag. She throws her purse over her shoulder and snatches it from me.

"Thanks for the ride," she says, her skin bunching up around her eyes.

"Nautica." I need to say something—to apologize.

Her hand flies up in my face to stop me, and she gives me a cold glare. "Don't. Just don't."

She whips around and heads up the porch steps. I lean back against my truck and wait until she goes in before leaving.

I feel like an asshole the entire three-minute drive to my house.

It's for the best, right?

nine

NAUTICA

I TOSS my bag onto the entryway floor and head into the kitchen to find my mom unloading groceries.

"Hi, sweetie," she greets, a bright smile on her face. She scurries around the island in her black flats to wrap me in a tight hug. "I've been counting down the days until I had both you and Simon home." She takes a step back to hold me at arm's length. "You look good. So much older."

I kiss her on the cheek, pull away, and laugh. "I've only been gone a few months. Not that much has changed."

"From a mother's standpoint, you have." She looks over my shoulder. "Did Bracken not come in?"

I'm unable to look her in the eyes—like she'll know what we did. "No, he needed to get home."

Her ruby-colored lips turn into a frown. "That's too bad. I baked some cookies to thank him for giving you a ride. I haven't seen him in so long."

"I'm sure he'll be here sometime during break." I give her a forced smile, hoping I'm wrong, but know I'm probably right.

He hangs out at our house more than he does his own. I

grab a cookie on the way to help her unpack the groceries, but she waves me away and tells me to sit down.

My mother is a beautiful woman. Her sandy brown hair is flowing in loose spiral curls. I can see a hint of mascara along her eyelashes. She takes care of herself well, but there's no mistaking that the loss of my father has taken a toll on her.

They were high school sweethearts. She got pregnant with Simon during their senior year. She dropped out to take care of him while my dad graduated and joined the military. Being a military wife was difficult, but she engrossed her life on being a good mother.

But being a good mother doesn't pay the bills. When he died, everything changed. Simon was fourteen. I was ten. She had no job, no work experience, or education, so it was hard for her to support us. Bracken's dad hired her at his dealership doing secretarial work, and she cleaned their house on the side for extra cash. He also worked around her school schedule when she decided to get her GED and then enrolled in community college to get a degree in medical coding. If it weren't for Bracken's family, our lives would've been much harder.

I head up to my room after catching up with her for a bit. I toss my bag onto my bed and am unpacking when my phone rings.

"Hello?" I answer.

"Hey girl," Macy sings out on the other line. "Did you make it home okay?"

"Yeah, Bracken dropped me off about an hour ago. We had to stay at a hotel last night because the roads were so bad."

She gasps dramatically. "You and him stayed in a hotel room alone together?" Her words come out slow.

"We did." I sit down and wait for the Macy freak out.

"Did you fuck him again?"

I stay silent. I don't want to go there right now. I'm still licking my wounds and pissed off.

"Holy shit, you did. I don't know whether to cheer for you or tell you you're an idiot for it."

"It was an accident. It wasn't supposed to happen."

"Yet, it continues to."

"I don't know what to do. It's not good for us, but it's like we can't stop now that we've started."

"Did you guys talk about it?"

"Not really. When he told me it wasn't going anywhere, I pretty much shut down the conversation. I wasn't in the mood to hear him say he basically used me. I might've punched him in the face or something."

"That's bullshit." She blows out a breath. "God, I could kick his arrogant ass right now. You wait until I get home. If I see him, I swear to God."

"Don't say anything to him. It's never happening again. Now, tell me what's going on with you?"

She talks about how bitter her parents are acting toward the other. Her mom spent the entire time Macy was there bitching about her dad and his new girlfriend. Macy sees their relationship as a lie and doesn't want to speak to them again.

"When are you coming home?" I ask.

"In a few days."

"Okay, I'll see you then."

"Figure shit out with Bracken before I come home or I'm kicking his ass."

ten

BRACKEN

TWO.

That's how many days I've been home. Two slow, long, and rough as hell days since I dropped off Nautica.

Three.

That's how many days it's been since I was last inside her, and it's fucking torture. I'm going crazy. She's taken me over like an illness I can't be cured of, and I'm not sure I want to be.

We haven't talked, but I've lost count of how many times I've picked up the phone to call her—only to chicken out each time. If she's not calling, I'm not calling. It's killing me but for the best.

Distance is key for our situation. I need to find a way to get my mind off her. I jacked off this morning thinking about how soft her skin felt against mine, and her begging moans haunted me last night. I feel like a damn high school kid again who got laid for the first time.

I hate that she compared herself to those other nameless chicks I've stuck my cock into. That's not true. Being with her was the best fuck I've ever had.

Simon texted me when he got home this morning. Relief washed through me, but tension built up in my muscles at the same time. Hanging out with him will most likely cut away at my hunger of wanting to fuck his little sister every second of the damn day, but I'm nervous he'll find out what I did.

I throw on a shirt before grabbing my phone to send him a text letting him know I'm on my way to pick him up for drinks. I've missed my best friend like fucking crazy, but guilt still consumes me.

What if Nautica told him?

What if I pissed her off so bad that she wanted revenge, and she knew the best way was to make me lose my best friend?

I never put anything past pissed-off women. I've had my fair share of them doing crazy shit to get back at me, mostly along the lines of fucking with my truck.

I snag my coat from my closet and head out of my bedroom. The house is quiet, but I know it isn't empty. I pass my parents' bedroom on the way to the stairs and abruptly stop when I see my mom sitting on the edge of their bed, tears falling down her cheeks. Seeing her this way isn't anything new, but it hurts every time.

"You alright, Ma?" I ask.

I've only seen her once since being home. She came downstairs to tell me hi, gave me a hug, ordered food, and then went back up to her bedroom. She's been caved up here ever since.

"You know I am, honey," she lies, sniffling while wiping her eyes.

I slide my hands into my pockets and rock back and forth on my heels. It's getting worse with each passing year, and I'm sure my absence is only making it harder—making her lonelier.

"Do you want to talk about it?" I ask.

Another sniffle. "No, I'll feel better after a nap." She opens her nightstand drawer and the sound of pills rolling from a bottle rings through our silence.

I'm not sure how many she swallows before giving me a fake smile and waving me out.

"Please shut my door," she says.

I take a step back and do as I'm told without another word. It's what I always do. I learned years ago to stop asking questions and let her make the rules. If she doesn't want to talk about it, there is no talking about it. My mom is as stubborn as I am. It makes me a shitty son to allow her to pretend, but there's nothing more I can do. You can't force someone who doesn't believe they have a problem to get help.

I tiptoe down the stairs, walk through the garage, jump into my truck, and head to Simon's place. I need that drink to clear my head. I actually need a few of 'em.

Not wanting to risk seeing Nautica, I wait in my truck and wait for Simon to come out. I need to get my head straight before I can face her in front of him.

"Bracken, dude, I've fucking missed you!" Simon shouts as the passenger door opens, and he gets in. "It's been too long."

I step on the gas pedal. "You have no fucking idea."

We bullshit with each other on the drive to the bar, and I hope they have something strong enough to make me forget about his sister.

"It feels good to have a drink," Simon says, grabbing his beer and taking a long swig. He wipes his mouth with his sleeve and grins. "Damn, I missed this shit."

We sit at a table across from each other. He's changed. The color of his hair still matches Nautica's, dark as the night, but the curls that once hit the bottom of his ears are gone—replaced with a shaved head. He's in the best shape he's ever been. The military is doing him good.

I take a long drink of my beer. "I bet. I can't imagine being stuck trudging through the damn snow while some drill sergeant screams at me for not making my damn bed right."

"I'm not going to lie. It's not fucking easy. But if my dad did it for our family, so can I. Plus, I feel like I'm doing something good, you know?" He's done everything to follow in his father's footsteps.

I nod. "Do you have any idea when they're shipping you overseas?"

"I'm supposed to leave for my tour next month."

I suck in my cheeks and rub the back of my neck. "Shit, that's too soon. Be careful, man. Please be careful."

"You know I will. I have to be here for my family." He leans back in his seat and sets his hands behind his head. "How's my little sister? Is she going wild out there?"

I suck down the remainder of my beer and signal to our waitress for another. "She hasn't been too bad. It's her freshman year, so you can expect her to get a little crazy, but she's called me anytime she needed a ride or anything." I grab the beer as soon as she hands it to me and take a drink to swallow down my bullshit.

He leans forward and slaps me on the back. "Thank you. I appreciate it, bro. I don't know what I'd do if she was out there alone. Thank fuck I can trust you with her. You know how college guys can be. They'll try to get in her panties and then never talk to her again."

He lifts his beer toward me, and I feel like an asshole when I tap mine against his.

* * *

I find my dad sitting in the kitchen with a drink in his hand when I get home from dropping Simon off. He holds up an expensive bottle of whiskey when he notices me standing in the dim light.

"You want a drink?" he asks.

I take a step forward. His eyes are glossy, letting me know this isn't his first glass.

I came in here for some water to help drown out my buzz, but the taste of liquor sounds more appetizing. Whiskey is just what the doctor ordered to wash Nautica from my thoughts because the beer is doing a pretty shitty job. Nothing has changed.

"Sure." I grab a glass from a cabinet, and he fills it up when I hand it to him. I sit down a few stools away from him and sip on my drink.

He plays with the glass in his hand. "It's good to have you home. I've missed you."

He's in his work suit. His black hair, peppered gray strands, is freshly cut and swept back with gel—the same hairstyle he's had for years. The gold watch I bought him for his birthday last year is wrapped around his wrist. He's missing his wedding ring.

"I've missed you, too," I say.

"Have you talked to your mother? Has she even left her bedroom today?"

I blow out a breath—not wanting to venture into this conversation. "She was down here when I got home but hasn't been out since."

"Shit," he hisses, shaking his head in disapproval. "We have a dinner tomorrow."

"I'm sure she'll be back to her old self by then."

She can pull herself together in minutes if it's for business or money. I don't know how the hell she does it.

"Temporarily," he mutters.

I can see the pain in his eyes. The subject makes him just as uncomfortable as it does me.

"How's school going?"

"Good. I can't wait to graduate. One more semester to go."

"I can't wait for you to be back here. You're the perfect man to take over the lot when I'm ready to retire." He downs his glass and pours another. "We do have some work to do."

"Work?"

He swallows down another drink and nods. "Yes, work. You need to start settling down. We need to find you a wife."

I almost drop my glass at his words. *That's not happening.*

"It looks better," he goes on. "Family men get more business. People like to buy shit from people with stability."

I shake my head. "A wife isn't in the cards for me anytime soon. I enjoy my freedom too much." I chuckle. "I haven't even graduated college yet."

He holds up his hand. "I get it, I get it. It was hard for me to settle down, but your shit has to be together to run a successful business. You don't need money-hungry floozies using you."

"Yeah, I'll think about it," I lie.

I stumble up the stairs to my bedroom after we've both passed the line of being tipsy. My dad heads toward the guest room. I shut my door, strip off my clothes, and fall face-first onto my bed. I eventually gain the strength to flip myself over when I hear my phone go off on my nightstand. I snag it and see a message from Kelly.

Kelly is a girl I occasionally fuck around with when I'm home. Her text tells me she's fully aware I'm here and wants to get together tomorrow night for a drink and a fuck.

I ignore her message and scroll through my Contacts. Only one name is on my mind. It's the one that shouldn't be. Ringing comes alive on the other end when I hit it.

Voicemail.

She either hit the ignore button or is asleep. I hope for the latter. I decide to leave her a message.

"Hey babe, it's me. Bracken." I hope my words aren't too slurred. "I'm sure you know that since it says my name. Anyway, I want to apologize. I can't stop thinking about you, and I don't want you to hate me. I was … shit … I am an idiot. I should've never allowed myself to touch you like that. I should've never fucking caved. The truth is, I've wanted you for so long. That night, it was like nothing else mattered but the two of us, and there were no consequences. I want it to happen again. I wish I could touch you … fuck you … again."

I hang up.

Then dial her again.

"It's me … again. I shouldn't have said that. Please erase that last message. I shouldn't tell you how much I fucking crave you, but I can't keep lying. I wanted to touch you so fucking bad. Shit, I still want to. I want to be back inside you." I glance down at my cock. "And fuck me, I'm hard as a rock just thinking about your pussy. Shit! Call me if you're still awake. I need you."

I hang up.

And call her back.

"It's me … again. I'm drunk and horny. If you're still awake, come over."

.   .   .

Click.

Short, simple, and straight to the point.

eleven

NAUTICA

"HI, *it's me again. Fuck. I shouldn't have said that shit, but I can't stop myself from blurting out the truth ... what I feel ... right now. It's just I want you so bad it's killing me. Physically killing me. I'm going to go jack off now. Bye.*"

I feel hot underneath my blanket, my body flushing with heat, as I clench my phone and listen to Bracken's voicemails from last night *for the third time.* I had my phone on silent, thank God. I don't know what I would've done if I'd answered and been given that proposal.

It would've most likely been along the lines of showing up with my panties in my hand and letting him have his way with me. No matter how much the man pisses me off, he never fails to turn me on.

He overtakes my train of thought. His touch and voice set me on fire. I should delete every message, but I can't. I'm keeping them so I can relieve myself to his drunken mistake as many times as I want.

I lower my hand down my stomach and underneath my

pajama shorts. My panties are wet. My heart races as I sluggishly rub my tiny nub. My soft fingertips brush along my sensitive spot. I stroke myself but imagine it's Bracken's finger doing the job for me. I shut my eyes, seeing his face and hearing his voice until my release shatters through me.

So much for the whole moving on thing.

* * *

Simon and my mom are in the kitchen eating breakfast when I walk in, post-Bracken's-voice-induced orgasm.

I know Simon and Bracken went out for drinks last night, and I'm pretty sure Bracken didn't drunkenly confess about us because Simon didn't come barging into my bedroom in a fit of anger.

"Good morning, dear sister," Simon says. He ruffles his fingers through my hair as he strolls past me.

Yep, he definitely doesn't know anything.

I swat his hand away. "You better not have bacon grease on those paws."

He falls down in the seat next to me. "Where did you run off to last night?"

"I went out with some friends." Some girls from high school invited me to a party, so I left before Simon got out of the shower. I didn't want to play the hundred questions game.

He cocks his head to the side. "You went out with some friends?"

I snag a piece of bacon from his plate. "Yes, in case you didn't know, I do have friends. Heather Scott had people over last night so everyone from our class could catch up."

Heather's is where I ran into the guy who'd been the quarterback of the football team. Quinton King. We had sophomore chemistry together and even made out once during a middle school game of Seven Seconds in Heaven. He's attending college in Kentucky, where he got a full-ride scholarship to play football. By the end of the night, we'd exchanged numbers, and he asked me to hang out before we both headed back to school. I said yes.

Maybe he'll move my attention away from Bracken, although I'm not sure how realistic that is. Bracken has consumed me for eleven years. It's hard to let something like that go.

I prepare myself to hear whatever lecture Simon is about to give on boys and parties.

"That's cool," he says with a shrug. He looks at our mom. "Bracken is coming over for chili tonight."

I almost fall out of my chair at the mention of his name *and* for the fact that Simon isn't pissed about me going out.

Did he trip and hit his head? My high school days were filled with dateless nights and unfair curfews. No proms. No staying out after midnight. Teenage boys didn't line up to date the girl whose brother threatened to kill them.

"Do you care if I have someone over too?" I ask my mom when a good idea bursts into my head.

Bracken has been playing me like a yo-yo. He's giving me a taste of whiplash, and I don't like it. He wants to be with me. He doesn't want to be with me. He wants us to stay away from each other. He leaves me voicemails begging me to come over. The man can't make his mind up, and he needs a taste of his own medicine.

"Who?" Simon asks, cutting in, the old him reemerging.

"Quinton King," I answer.

"Sure," my mom says, the word barely making it out of her mouth before Simon interrupts her.

"The kid from the football team?" he asks.

I nod.

He doesn't look elated at my response.

"Don't mess with him," I warn. "He's a nice guy."

He snorts. "There are no nice guys, little sister." He taps me on the tip of my nose. "You need to remember that before you do something stupid."

Too late.

"So you're not a nice guy?" I question, throwing his answer in his face.

"Would I want you to date a guy like me? Hell no."

"Not every guy is like you."

He scoffs. "Yes, they are. When you're thirty and meet a good man who drives a Honda or is in the military, then you can date him. But these college boys, *especially* college athletes, are not interested in anything serious. Trust me. I told you that before you left for school. I hope you haven't forgotten it."

I roll my eyes. "Yeah, yeah. You're always right."

He's going to fly off the handle if he ever finds out I slept with Bracken.

twelve

BRACKEN

I IGNORE three more of Kelly's calls and don't bother opening her texts. It's a jackass move, but it'd be a bigger jackass move if I fucked around with her.

There's too much chaos on my mind to be worrying about Kelly sucking my cock, like the fact that I just pulled up to Simon's house to have dinner with everyone, including his sexy little sister. I have to get my head on straight and play it cool.

I let out a ragged breath and rub my neck. I've been over here for dinner hundreds of times, but everything is different now. I have to go in there, take a seat across from her at the table, and stop myself from touching her. It's going to take all my restraint to hold back the mental images of her taking my cock while her mom tries to have a conversation with me. I already know shit isn't going to end well tonight if my dick has any say in it.

The savory smell of chili powder and cayenne pepper bombards my nostrils when I walk through the front door, not bothering to knock. I walk straight to the kitchen, where I hear laughing. I find Simon and his mom, Pamela. Nautica is nowhere in sight.

"There's my second son," Pamela greets when she sees me. She moves away from the stove to give me a hug. "I've missed having you over for dinner."

"Trust me, I've missed it just as much," I say, chuckling. "It sucks having to make your own meals. Thanks for having me."

She slaps me on the chest. "Oh, stop it. You know you're always welcome here."

Simon gets up from his chair. "Let's watch the game until the food is ready." He glances over at Pamela, whose attention is back on the stove. "You mind, Ma?"

She waves us away with a smile on her face. "No. You two go ahead. It's easier for me to work without Simon trying to stick his finger in the pot repeatedly."

I follow him into the living room. He flips on the TV. "Where's Nautica?" I ask, taking a look around. I'm trying to appear as casual as possible, but the question has been eating at me since I walked through the door.

Did she bail because she knew I was coming?

He lets out an agitated grunt and falls down in a chair. "Get this. She's upstairs in her room with some fucking dude." He tosses the remote down on the table roughly.

My pulse races, and I have to sit down. "She's what?"

How the fuck is Simon okay with this? The old him would be kicking out the asshole and putting Nautica in time-out.

His jaw clenches. "Yeah, I'm not too fucking happy about it. I guess she ran into some football player last night at a party and invited him over for dinner. I told her to keep her ass in the living room, but does she listen to me? Nope. Apparently, she thinks the rules don't apply to her anymore now that she's in college."

"Can't you tell them to come down here?" I don't know what would be worse: seeing her with him, or sitting here with the endless thoughts of what they could be doing up there.

Fucking, that's what. That's the only reason I'm ever in a chick's bedroom.

He shakes his head. "My mom sided with her." He mimics her voice. "She's eighteen now. That gives her more freedom."

I swallow down the anger boiling in the back of my throat. My cock was inside her only a few nights ago, and now she has some other dude in her bedroom? That's not fucking cool. She's going to hear about it.

My knees are bouncing. I want to charge up those stairs and ask her what the hell she thinks she's doing. No one else should be in her bedroom ... in her bed ... but me.

But I can't. My punishment is sitting here and acting normal, like this shit doesn't bother me. I have to suppress my anger and watch this stupid-ass game, which is easier said than done.

I grit my teeth. I can't wait until she gets her ass down here. She has some explaining to do.

Dinner is hell, to say the least, which sucks because I usually enjoy Pam's chili.

Nautica didn't come down until Pam texted dinner that was ready. By that time, I was on the verge of dragging her friend down the stairs and kicking his ass out. I needed to talk to her.

When they got down, I still didn't get the chance. Nautica didn't act surprised to see me, so she must've known I was coming. She's trying to make me jealous. I'm sure of it—and it's working. Douchebag stayed by her side, flirting with her nonstop. I'm surprised I didn't cough up my damn food.

My dad told me about him a few years ago. He was the only guy, other than myself, to make varsity his freshman year. Word is he received a scholarship to some hotshot college and is on his way to the NFL.

"Here, let me help you," I rush out. I slide my chair out and get up as soon as Nautica offers to clear the table. I grab my bowl, then Simon's, and follow her into the kitchen, my pulse spiraling with every step. I set the bowls down on the counter as soon as we make it into the kitchen and out of earshot of everyone.

"What the fuck do you think you're doing?" I whisper harshly. I gulp, watching her as she turns around, ignoring me, and starts to load the dishwasher. My fingernails dig into the edge of the counter. "Answer me." It's becoming harder to keep my voice down.

"I don't know what you're talking about," she answers, keeping her back to me. "*What I'm doing* is cleaning up after dinner, *obviously.*"

I take three long strides to her. My chest bumps into her back as I cage her between the sink and me. Her breathing quickens.

"Answer this, then. Why the fuck did you invite another guy over for dinner, and more importantly, have him in your damn bedroom?" I hiss in her ear. My fingers tightly wrap around her hips, and I push into her. "You knew I'd be here. Are you trying to torture me?"

She stays still, but I can feel the goose bumps rising along her skin. "Not that it's any of your business, but we were watching the game."

"And why couldn't you watch the game downstairs with everyone else? *With me?*"

I grunt and take a step back when her elbow slams into my stomach. "Maybe because I wanted some privacy. Damn, Bracken. You have no right to question me about what I'm doing." She shuts the dishwasher with her knee and keeps her distance from me.

"Privacy for what?"

She lets out a heavy sigh as her hands fall slack to her sides. "Quit being an asshole. I don't owe you answers. You're the one who blew *me* off. You're the one who fucked me *twice* and then said we were a bad idea."

I throw my arms out. "I didn't expect you to start blowing someone else a few days later."

I dodge a kitchen towel flying my way. "Fuck you," she spats. "I'm allowed to hang out with other guys. I'm sure you're not planning on keeping your dick in your pants while you're home. You probably have a *long* list of girls waiting to fuck you as soon as you leave here."

"I haven't touched anyone since you."

I notice a faint smile appear on her lips before she fights it off. "I appreciate that, but you don't want me, so it's okay. We're both free to do whatever we want. Oh, and don't leave me any more messages of you jacking off. They're annoying." Her hand smacks into my chest playfully before she saunters out of the kitchen, her hips swaying from side to side.

I lean back against the wall. She's playing mind games with me, fucking with me, and it's working.

I count to ten to calm myself down before I go back into the living room with Simon. Nautica must be back in her bedroom with lover boy. I fall on the couch. I'm not leaving until he does.

Twenty minutes pass until I hear footsteps coming down the stairs. I turn around to see Nautica and him walking outside.

Thank fucking God.

thirteen

NAUTICA

QUINTON TELLS me good night with a kiss on the cheek and a wave before climbing into his black, four-door Jeep.

He acted like the perfect gentleman tonight. He made no sly moves, no hand up the shirt maneuvers while we watched the game, nothing—which surprised me.

Like Bracken, he had the total man-slut reputation in high school. Girls threw themselves at him, and he was rumored to only date the ones who put out.

Apparently, I have a type.

But he'd been nothing but sweet. It might've been the fact that my brother and Bracken were downstairs cock-blocking him.

We went back upstairs after dinner to watch a movie and hang out. Even though I was still pissed about Bracken questioning me in the kitchen, Quinton helped take my mind off him. He told me about the overwhelming pressure football puts on him. I told him how refreshing the independence of being in college feels.

I wait until I can no longer make out his taillights before heading back inside. I know what's coming—an annoying interrogation from Simon. And Bracken is most likely going to join him since he finds it necessary to suddenly be in my business.

They're watching a movie in the living room. I quietly try to creep up the stairs to head back to my bedroom but have no luck.

"Hold it," Simon calls out.

I stop and look back at him.

"Did your new little boyfriend leave?" You can sense the sarcasm in his tone.

"Don't be an asshole," I mutter, flipping him off. "Or I'll invite him back over tomorrow."

"Sit your mean ass down and hang out with your big brother. I've missed you." He points at the open seat next to Bracken on the couch.

I stretch out my arms and fake a long yawn. "I would, but I'm actually feeling pretty tired. I've had a long night."

Bracken turns around to look at me. "A long night?" he asks with a raised brow. "What did you do that made it *so long?*" He's trying to hold back the venom in his tone because of Simon, but he isn't doing that great of a job at it.

I turn around and start to head up the stairs again, but he keeps talking.

"Oh come on, party pooper. It's only nine o'clock. Hang out with us now that your little *boyfriend* is gone."

I whip back around to face him. "He's not my boyfriend."

"You two sure looked awfully tight and cuddly."

"Then I'd suggest you get your eyes checked."

Simon's gaze whips back and forth between Bracken and me. He isn't used to hostility with us. Shit, I'm not used to it. We've always gotten along.

"Fine," I say around a groan. "But I'm only staying for a while."

The last thing I need is Simon suspecting something, so I walk into the living room and plop down on the couch, as far away from Bracken as possible. Unfortunately, our couch isn't that big.

I glance over at Bracken briefly and become annoyed at the giant smirk on his face. The asshole loves getting his way.

I survive an hour with them and Bracken's subtle touches before faking another yawn. "I'm headed to bed," I tell them, getting up. I've had enough. An hour is adequate time to prove my innocence. Now, I need to get the hell out of here.

"Good night, sis," Simon calls out, not looking away from the TV.

Bracken stays quiet. Thank God.

I turn on my TV and climb into bed when I get to my room. An hour passes, and my phone chimes with a text from Bracken.

I open it.

Bracken: I'm about to leave.

I hit the reply button.

Me: Okay? Bye.

Bracken: Where's my kiss good night?

The nerve of this asshole.

I take a deep breath and hold back the impulse of marching down the stairs and giving him a slap good night. *Who the hell does he think he is?* He can't play games with me like that.

I slam my finger down on the reply button.

Me: I've already given someone a kiss good night. Thanks anyway.

I'm lying, but so what? He needs to feel bad for basically telling me I don't mean shit to him and blowing me off. I want him to experience the same jealousy I've had for years.

Bracken: Don't fuck with me, Nautica.

I toss my phone down next to me, fully prepared to ignore

him for the rest of the night ... or forever if I can help it. I need to move on from my Bracken obsession.

I jump at the sound of my ringtone.

Bracken *again.*

I focus on the screen and watch his name flash, contemplating whether to answer.

"What?" I hiss, caving in.

"Are you ignoring me?" he asks.

"Sure am."

"And why the fuck are you doing that?"

I scoff. "Why do you think?"

I can hear the sound of his truck running in the background. Then it goes silent. "Come over."

"Come over?"

"Yes. Come over. I want to see you."

"Have you been drinking? I can't come over to your house."

"Why not? I'm outside waiting in my truck. Come over. We'll go inside, go for a ride, something. I want to see you."

I look at my alarm clock. "It's almost midnight."

"And? Do you plan on turning into a pumpkin or some shit?"

"No, smart-ass. What I'm saying is that I can't go downstairs and tell Simon I'm going to your house to hang out."

"Simon went to bed. Sneak out."

"Good night."

It takes every ounce of my willpower to hang up on him.

Games. The man always wants to play games.

I groan when my phone beeps with another message.

A picture message.

A dick pic, specifically.

Holy fucking shit!

His pants are pulled down, and his hand is wrapped around

the base of his cock. My mouth flies open, and my phone slips straight through my fingers, hitting me in the face.

I snatch my phone back up when another text comes.

Him again.

Bracken: Come see it in person.

I hit reply.

Nautica: You've lost your damn mind. Go to bed.

Bracken: That's not going to happen because I can't stop thinking about you. Come over. I'll make it worth your while. I promise.

My nerves stir, and my body grows hotter when I pull the picture back up on my phone. I gulp, but can't break my eyes away from his cock. Anticipation and need beg at my core. I can't believe I'm getting this excited from looking at a fucking dick selfie.

I slide out of bed and grab my coat and boots. I can hear Simon's TV from his bedroom as I tiptoe down the stairs. I quietly slip out the front door and into the cold night.

Holy shit. I'm sneaking over to Bracken's house for a booty call or whatever it is that we're going to be doing.

I walk down the sidewalk carefully so I don't bust my ass on the ice. His truck is parked in the driveway but isn't running. I pull out my phone from my coat pocket.

Me: I'm outside.

Panic runs through me as I take a look around. *What if he was only messing around with me? What if this is all a joke, and he hadn't actually expected me to show up?*

I start to back away until the driver's side door of his truck flies open. I pull my coat tighter around my body and walk up the driveway to meet him.

"You actually came," he says, his eyes wide in disbelief.

I'm standing only a few inches away from him as my heart

races. "Yeah," I mutter. I take a nervous step back, but he grabs my arm to stop me before I make a run for it.

"Whoa, whoa. Where do you think you're going?"

I shiver as his finger runs up and down my hand. "I'm not in the mood for your games tonight. It's fucking freezing out here."

He drops my hand and scrunches up his face. "Games? Do you think me inviting you over here is a fucking game?" He steps underneath the floodlights and points between his legs.

My hand goes to my mouth as I look down and eye the hard bulge underneath his jeans.

"Nothing about the two of us is a game, nor will it ever be. Is it confusing as fuck? Yes. Is it hard for me? Absolutely, and in more ways than one." He grins, and I slap his shoulder. "But never a game. I asked you to come here because I had to see you, or I'll go fucking crazy all night."

I shiver and stare at him, speechless. I'm not sure how to respond. His hand reaches out to brush away the snowflakes on my face. I gasp when his lips meet mine. Unlike our other forbidden kisses, this one is soft, slow, and sweet. *It's nice.*

"Come inside," he says, cocking his head toward his house.

"What about your parents?" I ask.

"They're passed out. Plus, I doubt they'd care if you come in."

I look from the house and then back to his truck. "What about your truck?"

He gives me a sideways look when I take a step back and open the back door.

"Are you serious? We'll freeze our asses off."

I smile. "Let's warm each other up, shall we?"

I slide into the back seat without giving him the chance to reply. *How the hell is this happening? How have I gone from being a nervous wreck to being a seductress luring him into the back seat of his truck?*

"Why can't I stay away from you?" he asks, appearing in the doorway.

"The same reason I can't stay the hell away from you. It's stupid for us to keep denying what feels so right."

He doesn't move. "I don't want to fuck you in the back of my truck." He shakes his head, refusing to look at me. "It's not right."

"Why not?"

"You're better than that. You deserve more."

I smack my hand against the seat. "Do you know how hot this big, badass machine is? I've been dreaming about you taking me in this back seat for years. On the night of your graduation party, I was silently praying for you to come to your senses, pull over, and have your way with me back here. If there's anywhere I'd like for you to fuck me, it's here."

"Motherfucker, that's the hottest thing anyone has ever said to me." The door slams shut, taking away our source of light, but I can sense his body heat moving in close. "I want you to ride my cock again. Ride me as fucking hard as you wanted to fuck me that night."

I can hear the jingle of his belt unbuckling, along with the faint sound of his zipper tearing down. I shiver as I do the same thing. I take a deep breath before climbing over to him as soon as my panties are off. I wrap my hand around his hard cock.

"Is this what you wanted me to come over and do?" I whisper against his lips. "Is this why you sent me that dick pic?" I'm not sure where this dirty-talking girl is coming from, but I like it. My words are electrifying, exciting me as much as they are him. My head falls back when he snakes his hand into my hair and pulls it.

"Fuck yes," he groans out. "Jack me off, but I want to get off inside your pussy. Not on your hand."

I casually stroke him a few times before positioning myself over his lap. I cry out in ecstasy when his cock fills me. My entire body trembles as I slam all my weight down on him. With each plunge, he grips my ass and slaps it, harder and rougher each time.

This is what I've wanted for years. My fantasies are finally coming alive. My only fear is what's going to happen when I wake up.

* * *

"You can sleep here tonight if you want," Bracken says, buckling his pants while I start to get dressed.

After we both got off, we grabbed our clothes and hopped into the front seat so Bracken could turn the heat on.

I throw my shirt on. "That won't be obvious or anything," I answer, around a laugh. He's afraid of Simon finding out about us, so I don't understand why he'd invite me to stay overnight.

"Tell them you stayed over at a friend's."

"And left in the middle of the night?" I shake my head. "I wish I could, but I have to go."

Nothing sounds better than climbing into his bed and feeling his arms wrap around me, but we can't risk it. I'm not ready to lose him yet.

I jump out of his truck, and he joins me outside.

"I'll walk you," he says, grabbing my hand and leading me toward my house.

We stroll down the sidewalk, snow crunching beneath our feet, and hold hands in silence. He stops at the front door and turns me to face him. He draws back and becomes quiet.

"What?" I ask.

"This is … it's crazy," he says, a small laugh escaping him.

"What is?"

"Our time together … every night … it's like it's competing for my favorite one."

My breath catches as he runs his fingers along my cheeks. That is the last thing I expected him to say. This Bracken, this sweet Bracken, is going to keep bringing me back for more, even though I'm fully aware it's not a good idea.

"Thank you for coming over," he says.

I grin. "Thank you for the orgasm."

He chuckles. "Anytime, babe. Any-fucking-time." His lips smack into my forehead. "Sweet dreams."

fourteen

NAUTICA

"SO WHAT'S GOING on with you and asshole?" Macy asks me over the phone. "Any new updates I should know about?"

"I don't even know," I answer.

It's the day after I snuck over to Bracken's. I haven't heard from him yet, and I'm not sure whether to text him. I don't want to look too needy or desperate. I'm playing the torturing game of waiting until he texts me, but I hope he isn't doing the same thing.

I sit down and think about last night. The way he held me, kissed me, walked me home, all those sweet, little gestures are making me fall harder and harder for him. And he has no idea.

"Earth to Nautica," Macy calls out, and I give her my full attention. "What do you mean you don't know?"

"We keep having sex—like *way* too much sex, and we can't seem to stop doing it."

She laughs. "There's no such thing as too much sex."

"You know what I mean. Too much sex between people who shouldn't be having sex. That's a problem."

She snorts in response.

"What?"

"I'm not sure why you're both so caught up in the whole *'we shouldn't be having sex'* thing. I mean, who made the rule that you can't sleep together because he's your brother's best friend? It's ridiculous. You're both adults who like to screw each other, who cares? Stop letting other people get in your way."

I smile in agreement. Macy is right. I'm a big girl. I'm old and smart enough to decide who I screw. Whether it's a short-term thing or a relationship, nobody else should decide that for me.

fifteen

BRACKEN

"HEY THERE, SON," my dad greets when I walk into his office. He asked me to stop by the dealership and look at the renovations he's been working on for the past few months.

Casey Auto Sales is the largest car dealership in our county. My dad started it twenty years ago with only eight cars on the lot. Now, there are around a hundred. He's spent countless hours working his ass off to grow his company and even managed to open a few more locations in other towns. Our plan is me following in his footsteps, possibly open a few more, and take over the reins when he retires, which I have no problem doing. I've been working at the dealership since I was fifteen.

"The place looks good," I tell him, signaling to the show-room behind us before shutting his office door. "I didn't know Pamela was working here again." I was surprised to walk in and see her sitting behind the front desk helping a customer.

"She started back around six months ago. With Simon and Nautica both gone, she gets lonely. Not to mention, she also has to pay what the scholarship doesn't cover of Nautica's tuition," he explains.

I take my own seat in the uncomfortable customer chair. "That's nice of you to help her out."

I've always admired that my dad is willing to help people—whether it be my best friend's family, one in need of food, or sponsoring families for the holidays. He's a very charitable man.

"And don't forget the company holiday party is tonight," he reminds me.

I frown, letting out a long groan. "Come on, don't make me go to that shit. You know I'm not a fan of those."

I used to be, but then I was caught banging one of his secretaries in the parking lot a couple of years ago. My dad was pissed and told me if I did it again, he'd fire the chick. It's difficult trying to concentrate on fucking a woman when you're worried she might be unemployed the next day because she wanted your cock.

He points a pen my way. "You're coming," he insists. "It will look good. You'll be here full-time next year." He waggles his eyebrows. "I'll even let you bring a date ... just please don't let it be one of my employees. This town is full of women, and the whole fraternizing thing isn't a good way to start."

I tap my foot. "Fine. I'll be there."

"Great, and don't forget to make sure your suit still fits." He stops me when I turn around to leave. "And please check on your mother for me, will you? She's supposed to be here tonight."

"Sure, no problem."

I say hi to a few people before leaving. I pull out my phone to text Nautica as soon as I get back in my truck.

Me: You up for a party tonight?

My phone beeps with her reply.

Nautica: Elaborate.

Me: The dealership's Christmas party is tonight. Come with me?

Nautica: Are you asking me out on a date?

I hesitate, not sure how to answer.

Me: Yeah ... something like that.

A date.

I've never been on a real date. I'm taking a huge risk and going against my better judgment, but I can't stop myself. If I go to the party solo, I'll be fighting off chicks because there's no way anyone who's not Nautica interests me, and there's no way I can stomach having anyone else but her on my arm.

This girl, she's getting the best of me. She's consuming me, and I need to find a way to stop it before we get in too deep.

I'll think about that later. I'm giving myself one more night of her and will call shit off tomorrow.

* * *

"Shit, man, I didn't know we had plans tonight," Simon says in surprise when he opens his front door. "And what's with the fancy-ass penguin suit? I'm honored you want to look nice for me and all, but this is a little too much. I prefer guys in leather jackets."

I push him back and walk inside. "Don't flatter yourself. I'm not hanging out with your ugly ass tonight. You're not my type. Nautica is coming to the dealership's holiday party with me," I explain.

He edges in closer, making me nervous, and his brows furrow together. "Did you just tell me you're taking my sister out on a date?"

"No, dumbass. Do I need to buy you a hearing aid for Christmas? It's the dealership's holiday party. You know we have one every year." I slap his shoulder. "You're more than welcome to tag along. I can always use more company. The more, the merrier, but you have to wear a tie."

My smart-ass comment hides the fact that I'm bluffing. I'm praying he doesn't actually decide to come. Talk about a cock-block.

"Funny asshole, but I have plans."

"Plans? What kind of plans?"

We live in a small town where not much shit happens. If something was going on tonight, I'd know about it.

He shrugs and turns his attention to the stairs. "I'm just hanging out with someone. It's not a big deal."

"*Someone?* And who is this secret someone?"

"You don't know her."

"I know everyone in this town. It's so fucking small. I swear you can stretch my balls across the county lines."

"She's not from around here. She's visiting her friend or some shit." His face tightens, and he can't look me in the eyes.

"You're hiding something." I cock my head to the side, waiting for him to tell me what the hell it is.

"Dude, you're being paranoid. Take my sister to the party. She needs to get out, but don't let her drink and keep an eye on her, okay?"

I shut up. He isn't the only one hiding something, so I'm apprehensive about pushing too much. I don't want shit turning on me. As long as this mystery chick keeps him occupied enough not to realize who I'm sticking my dick into, I'm keeping my damn mouth shut.

"You know I got her. Always."

He slaps me on the back. "That's why you're my best friend. You look out for her as much as I do."

His words hit me with force, making me feel like an even bigger bastard.

"Is that Bracken?" Nautica calls from up the stairs.

My stomach jolts with nervousness. *Act cool. Act fucking cool.*

"Yes!" Simon yells at her. "So, get your ass down here. I need to lay down some ground rules."

"What the hell do you mean lay down the rules?" I ask with a snarl, looking at him. "You sound like a fucking idiot. You're not her father in some Nicholas Sparks book."

He throws his head back in laughter. "Screw you. I fucking love *The Notebook*. My mom and Nautica have made me watch that movie so many damn times. I could probably recite it word for word."

"Figures," I mutter, but zone out from our conversation when I hear shuffling come from the top of the stairs. I remind myself to breathe when I see Nautica come down, step-by-step in what seems like slow motion. I move around, telling my cock to calm down as she tortures me.

She looks breathtaking. Her black hair is down, parted in the middle, and flowing in loose curls. A sparkly red dress hugs every curve of her delicious body and stops at her knees. Perfect fuck-me black high heels make her seem inches taller. Her lips are bright red. I can't wait to taste them.

I'm trying to hide how turned on I am from Simon, but he's not an idiot. There's no way he missed my jaw practically hitting the ground.

"You better not be eye-fucking her, man," he hisses, pushing my shoulder.

I shove him back. "Chill the fuck out. Tonight is strictly platonic."

I wait until I put her in my truck and get in before saying anything even though I'm bursting to tell her how I feel. "I have to start off tonight by telling you how fucking sexy you look," I say, turning the key, and the ignition fires on. "I'm not sure if I'm going to be able to keep my hands off you. The only thing I can focus on right now is ripping that dress off your body, putting you in the back seat, and feeling those heels bite into my back, giving me marks that'll stay there for days."

I notice the blush rise along her cheeks. "Thank you." She runs her hands down her dress. "That's exactly the reaction I was hoping for."

Fuck. I hope I can at least keep my hands off her while we're in public. I'll find a place to fuck her later because that is definitely happening tonight.

The parking lot is jam-packed, which was expected. Our holiday parties are always a crowded event. They're hosted at the main dealership, the first and largest one. They move out all the showroom cars and bring in caterers and a DJ. Every employee, from managers to the salespeople to the janitors from all three dealerships, is invited. My dad's most important advice he's ever given me for a thriving business is to make sure you have happy employees.

I jump out of my truck, hand the valet my keys, and open the passenger door. Nautica's hand interlaces with mine, and I lead her through the front doors.

"Your mom, is she coming tonight?" I ask her.

"Not that I know of. I think she's going to dinner with my aunt or something," she says, taking a look around. "Wow, this is amazing. It doesn't even look like the dealership."

All eyes are on us as if we're making some big-ass entrance. She tries to yank her hand out of mine, but I tighten my grip. She's not leaving my side tonight. I'm staking my claim. There are too many guys here—too many to try to take what's mine.

"Son, I see you found yourself an impressive date," a loud voice calls out.

I look up to see my parents heading our way. He snags a flute of champagne from a waiter. My mom is latched to his side like a second skin. She looks completely in her element—a different person than what I found this morning when I went to check on her. She'll do her act here, play her role, and then lock herself back in her bedroom for the next few days. That's how it always works.

Her long auburn hair is wrapped in a ponytail at the base of her neck, and a long, white gown runs down her body and hits the floor. Her makeup is professionally done. She looks happier than she actually feels.

"Nautica, darling, you look absolutely beautiful," she compliments, giving her a sweet smile. "I adore that dress on you."

My dad nods in agreement. When I was in high school, he told me on numerous occasions to scoop her up before some other lucky bastard did. He didn't understand that I couldn't cross that line.

"Thank you," Nautica replies, giving them a bright smile. "I'm excited about being here. I've never been before."

"My son slacks on asking pretty women on dates," my dad replies, opportunity lighting up in his eyes. "But it looks like he's doing much better."

My mom talks to her about school until my dad's CFO comes over and steals their attention away with business talk. Nautica hooks her elbow through mine, and we make a lap around the room. I say hey to a few guys I went to school with and try to steer clear of any chicks I've fucked, which is a challenge. It's like my dad has hired every women I've screwed.

I grab a glass of champagne, and we move to a corner of the room, away from the crowd. "You do realize that every man's eyes are on you, right?" I ask, coming up behind her and whispering those words in her ear.

Her back straightens when I wrap an arm around her waist. Her breathing labors. "You do realize that every woman's eyes are on you?" she counters.

"Their eyes are on me because they're jealous of how stunning you look in that dress, and they know all the dirty things I'm going to do to you later."

I drag my fingertips down her arm. I can't hold myself back from touching her any longer. My eyes stray to her ass. I lightly grab it and bite my lip to suppress a groan. This can't wait anymore. I have to have her.

My hand stays on her ass as I move my tongue along her earlobe. "Come with me," I say, my voice gravelly.

She attempts to turn around and look at me, but I don't allow it. "What … where?" she stutters.

"Just trust me."

I snag her hand in mine. She keeps up with me as I head toward a vacant office and slam the door shut. It's the one I chose to be mine when I start working here.

"Bracken," she whispers, looking from the door to me. "We … we can't do this *here.*"

I slide my hands down her back and grip her ass, bringing her into me roughly. "Oh yes, we can," I say. "There's no way I can stand here with you looking that damn good and keep my hands off you any longer. You have to give me a little taste, *something*, to hold me over before I take you somewhere and give it to you like I want. Hard, fast, and dirty."

Her lips go to my neck, sucking hard. "Then have your way with me, Mr. Casey. Fuck me in this office."

Fuck. No other words have made me harder in my life.

I turn her around, push her forward, and bend her over the desk. "Oh trust me, I'm going to do more than just have my way with you." I loosen my belt and unbuckle my pants.

"Prove it."

My pants fall to my ankles as I roughly tug up her dress. I get a good view of her plump, round ass and smack it. It fits perfectly in my hand. She shivers underneath the weight of my body.

I plunge into her with no warning. My hand cups her mouth at the same time a high moan slips through her lips. I draw in and out of her over and over again, getting rougher and faster with each pump. I hold her tight, not letting her move. She's practically pinned to the desk.

Perspiration films at the top of my forehead. Her breathing is ragged. Our bodies are growing more exhausted with every thrust and moan.

Damn, this is a workout. The best fucking workout I've ever had.

* * *

"I've been trying to call you."

I look up at the sound of the recognizable voice to find Kelly standing in front of me, a look of disappointment burned on her face.

I'm out of it. My brain is delirious, and I'm unable to think about anything but the amazing sex I just had. I stepped out of the office a few minutes ago while Nautica scurried off to the bathroom to clean herself up. I'm not sure how long we'd been gone or were screwing, but it was long enough that we were both a sweaty, panting mess.

"I've been busy," I answer. I still haven't returned a call or text from her. My mind has been on other shit.

She pulls her plump, shiny lips together. "I see that," she says sarcastically before letting out a laugh. "The best friend's little sister. Very classy, Bracken."

My stance straightens. *Shit.* Are we that obvious?

"I have no idea what you're talking about." I glance around for Nautica, trying to play it coy, but I know better. Kelly is a smart and perceptive woman. She was valedictorian of our class.

If I weren't caught up with Nautica at the moment, I probably would've been fucking her in that office, to be honest. She's a good lay, and there is no denying how attractive she is. She's standing only inches away from me in high heels and a black dress that shows off her ample cleavage. Her straight brown hair tumbles around the outside of each breast.

"Friends who are banging," she argues, smacking my shoulder when I give her a look. "Don't insult my intelligence. I'm a sexual relations major. I know when two people are fucking, and you two people *are fucking.*" She points at the office we just christened. "Not to mention, I just watched her race to the bathroom, her head down, hair a mess, and dress wrinkled. A few seconds later, you come strolling out with a satisfied look on your face." She swings her glass from side to side and stares at me, long and hard. "Does Simon know?"

"There isn't shit to know," I fire back.

"Whoa, settle down, killer. I'm not going to say anything. I don't want you to hate me because when you and Little Miss Innocent end things, which I know will happen, I don't want you cutting my ass off from good cock. I want you to come back to me." She takes a sip. "I'm probably more exciting, anyway."

She has no idea how much better Nautica is in and out of bed than she is, but I choose to keep that to myself. Kelly can be the grenade that blows us up. Keeping my cool with her is mandatory.

"How are you not a man?" I ask around a chuckle.

She downs the rest of her champagne and laughs. "Trust me when I say this isn't the first time I've been asked that question." She pats me on the back. "Be good, and let's pray Simon doesn't kill you when he finds out. It would be a waste of a perfect body."

She disappears before Nautica makes her way back to me.

sixteen

NAUTICA

"LATE NIGHT?" Macy asks.

I groan as she strolls into my bedroom and rips open the curtains. I cringe, trying to get accustomed to the sunlight beaming through. She got home sometime yesterday, and we have plans to hang out and go shopping today.

"I guess you can say that," I mutter, a yawn coming next. *More like a rough night*—considering how hard Bracken fucked me.

She stops at the end of my bed and looks at me. Her blond hair is neatly straightened, her lips a bright red. "And what exactly did this night consist of?" She already knows the answer. She's trying to be a pain in my ass, per usual.

I rise up and stretch out my arms. "I went to the dealership's holiday party, *remember?*"

"Oh yeah, with your little fuck buddy, Bracken. How did that go?"

I give her a dirty look, and she laughs. "Be careful saying that shit," I hiss. "If Simon hears you, we're all done for."

The mattress shakes when she crashes down next to me. "You need to tell Simon to get the hell over it. You're a grown woman. You're in college, and you can't stay single forever." She lets out a huff. "I mean, *he* thinks he can go out and screw everyone, but keeps a tight leash on you? That isn't fair, and you know it. It's time you put your foot down."

"I know, but I'm not only protecting myself. I'm looking out for Bracken, too. I don't want to go and tell Simon without making sure he's okay with it."

"Bracken doesn't need protecting. He needs to grow some balls and set Simon straight. He's a big boy."

I'm afraid to stir the pot after my night with Bracken, but we need to talk. Maybe last night was a reality check that we'd be good together. Simon seemed fine with us going to the party.

I snag my phone from my nightstand and notice two texts. One is from Bracken. The other from Quinton. They both say pretty much the same thing. *Good morning, beautiful.* I curse when my phone is ripped out of my hand.

"Damn," Macy draws out, her eyes scanning the screen. "Look at you, playgirl. You went from having no boyfriend to having two in only a few days. Go, best friend. That's my best friend."

I reach for my phone and snatch it from her. "Neither one of them is my boyfriend, thank you very much."

"So what are you going to do?" She rests her head on my shoulder. "I mean, no offense to Bracken, your one true love and all that shit, but I can't see much going forward with him, to be honest. He's too worried about your brother hating him. Plus, I'm pretty sure dude is a commitment-phobe."

My stomach sinks at the validity of her statement. I shut my eyes and remember last night. The way he rushed me into the office and lost his control, and then our second round in his truck before he took me home. My longing for him is becoming stronger with every kiss and screw.

But am I thinking our late-night screws mean more than

they should? Is this just a fling? He leaves me with too many uncertainties.

"God, I don't know what the hell to do," I tell her. "If I had to pick one of them to be with right now, you already know my choice would be Bracken. Unfortunately, like you said, I'm not sure if that's even an option."

She lifts her head. "If Bracken doesn't commit, it'll only verify he's as big as a dumbass as I think he is." She stands and holds out her hand. "Now, get your confused ass up. I'm starved. We can talk about your boyfriends over pancakes."

* * *

I walk through the front door with Macy to find Bracken and Simon in the living room.

"Hey, guys," Macy calls out. She tosses her shopping bags on the floor and falls down on the couch next to Simon. She slaps his arm when he dramatically scoots away from her.

"Hey, sis," he says, giving me a wave. He looks over at Macy and frowns. "And Macy. What are you two hell-raisers up to tonight?" He whips around to look at me. "And don't think because your little bad-influence sidekick is home that you can go out and act a fool."

"Screw you, Simon," Macy says, flipping him in the head. "You're only jealous that I'm not a fucking prude like you. You need to loosen up."

I tune out their arguing back and forth and sit down in a chair. I refuse to look at Bracken. I haven't texted him back yet because I'm trying to get my head straight. I need to distance myself until we can talk about where this is going.

"We're actually planning on going ice-skating." I hear Macy tell Simon. "Totally PG. Do you guys want to come?"

Simon hesitates for a moment, surprising me. I figured

she'd be answered with an immediate, "*Fuck no,*" as soon as he heard her question. He never hangs out with us, and he openly expresses how he can't handle being around Macy.

"Oh, come on, it'll be fun," she goes on. "And FYI, if you don't come, we're inviting other guys. I'm sure *Quinton* and some of his friends would be up for hanging out with us. Last chance before we ask them."

She shrugs innocently when I give her a dirty look. I'm planning on strangling her when we're alone. I still can't look at Bracken, but I could feel his eyes narrow at me when Macy said Quinton's name.

"Ice-skating doesn't sound too bad," Bracken says. "I mean, we don't have shit to do tonight." All the blood drains from my face at his answer. *He can't be serious?* He's actually going to put us in the firing pit of Simon? He's losing his mind.

"Fine," Simon replies around a groan. "But we're stopping and getting some food. I'm starving."

Macy jumps up from the couch. "We'll meet you down here in thirty minutes." She grabs my hand and drags me upstairs.

"Have you lost your damn mind?" I ask, slamming my bedroom door shut behind us.

She crosses her arms. "You're welcome," she replies.

"You're welcome for what? Setting me up for disaster?"

"No, you're welcome for helping you figure shit out. I'll keep Simon occupied."

I give her a blank look, and she slaps my arm.

"Not like that, perv. Not all of us have active sex lives right now. I'll talk to him and keep his mind off you and Bracken."

"Okay?" I draw out, still confused.

"I want to see how Bracken acts around the both of you. I need a firsthand experience so I can give advice."

"This won't end well." I point at her. "And when it blows up in our faces, you better help me fix it."

She flicks her hand through the air. "Nothing is going to blow up, drama queen. We need to figure out if Bracken is wasting your time."

"Let's hope Simon doesn't find out before we want him to."

I change my shirt and put on some makeup before heading back downstairs.

"Who's driving?" Bracken asks.

"You can," Simon answers. "Your truck has more space."

Macy giggles, and everyone looks at her. "I bet there's a lot of things of Bracken's that are bigger than yours," she says.

Simon shoots her a murderous glare. "Keep talking shit, Macy. See where the fuck it gets you," he fires back. "Your ass will be walking home from the rink."

My jaw drops as I watch their exchange. *What the?* I know they don't like each other, but it's never been this bad. I look over at Bracken, and he just shrugs.

"Shit, let me go grab my coat," Simon says, bumping into Macy's side as he dashes upstairs.

Macy looks at Bracken. "Have you had your back seat cleaned?" she asks him.

"No," he draws out. "Why?"

"Because I don't want to sit in your guys' sex juices."

His gaze swings to me. "You told her?" he questions, irritated. "She's got the biggest damn mouth in town."

"Of course, she told me, dumbass," Macy replies. "You think she can keep something like that from me? Nope." She gestures my way. "The girl has sex written all over her."

"Macy," I whisper harshly, ignoring the evil eye coming from Bracken, and tip my head toward the staircase.

She rolls her eyes. "I'm going to start calling your brother Ray Charles. The guy doesn't see shit that's right in front of him."

Just as I figured, this isn't going well. We haven't even left the house yet, and it's already a fiasco.

We pile into Bracken's truck. Bracken and Simon take the front while Macy and I get in the back. Macy sticks out her tongue dramatically as we climb into the back seat. I shove her before pulling the seat belt across my body. I run my hand across the soft leather as Bracken takes off, remembering every detail of our nights in here.

Damn you, Bracken Casey, for giving me everything I've dreamed of since I was a little girl and showing me that you can make me happy. Damn you for not making me any promises, confusing the shit out of me, and leaving me in the dark.

* * *

"I'm trying to act as normal as possible right now, but it's challenging," Bracken says quietly. He falls down next to me on the metal bench while I start to untie my skates.

I pull my left skate off. "Tell me about it," I say with a sigh. "I feel so paranoid, like he expects something when he probably has no idea."

So far, ice-skating has been an interesting event. We went to dinner first. Pizza. I wanted to strangle Macy the entire time. She was trying her damnedest to make everything uncomfortable as hell.

When we got to the pizzeria, she squeezed into the booth next to Simon before he could stop her, resulting in Bracken having to sit next to me. I can't be mad at her, though. She might have a sucky way of doing it, but I know she's only trying to help. She was the one who kept the conversation flowing. It wasn't necessarily *good* conversation, considering it consisted of her mainly talking about the parties we've gone to since arriving at KU, but it erased the awkward silence. She and

Simon spent the rest of the time arguing about stupid shit while Bracken and I sat quietly.

Bracken gets down on one knee and helps me take off my other skate. My heart skips a beat. The last time he'd done this was in his bedroom our first night—our first time.

"I know," he says. "This whole sneaking around shit isn't fun."

I look down at him. "Then maybe we should stop," I reply. I'm shocked at myself for even suggesting it, but I think Macy is getting to me. I need to find out where Bracken's head is. We either need to move forward or move on.

His face pales. He grabs the bottom of the bench to bring himself up and sits back down. "Stop hooking up?"

I take a calming breath. "Or stop hiding."

He takes off his black beanie to run his hands through his thick hair. "You know that isn't an option."

"And why not?" I let out an aggravated huff. "Are you really that terrified of my brother?" Simon is built and all, but Bracken has at least fifteen pounds on him. "Yeah, he'll probably be pissed in the beginning, but he'll get over it. It won't kill him."

"It has nothing to do with me being afraid of Simon. It's not that. It's just ..."

"It's what?" I cut off his bullshit reply because I know it's going to piss me off. Whenever we attempt to have a conversation with our clothes on it always turns ugly.

"Why can't we wait a little longer? Let's see how this break plays out before we tell him, okay?"

I scoot away as nausea builds up in my stomach. "I get it," I say through clenched teeth. "You don't want to tell him because it would be a waste, right?"

He looks at me in confusion. "What?"

"I'm not dumb. You're not actually planning on *being* with

me. You want to fuck me but not date me. You'll never change. So let's end it now. It's better this way."

He's shaking his head with his eyes down to the ground. "That's not what I meant. Those aren't my intentions."

"Then explain to me what I got wrong." I'm on the verge of tears. *Breathe ... breathe ... don't let him know he's hurting you.*

"It's just—"

"Are you guys already done?" Simon asks, coming up and interrupting us. When I told them I wanted to take a break, he and Macy stayed on the ice, and Bracken offered to come back with me. "Dude, I planned on showing your ass up." He looks over at Bracken with a competitive smile.

Bad fucking timing, brother.

"Let's see what you got then, asshole," Bracken says, bringing himself up. He doesn't look at me once as he walks away with him and heads toward the ice.

"Something just happened," Macy says, taking his spot. "I'm pretty sure we walked in on something, and from the looks of it, it wasn't something pretty." She stares at me, her eyebrows drawn together, while she waits for me to tell her the scoop.

I scrub my hands over my face and release a heavy sigh. "I'm wasting my time with him," I tell her. My voice loses power at the end. I want to fade in the background and disappear from here.

She releases a heavy sigh. "I was afraid of that, but at least we know his intentions now." Her shoulder bumps into mine. "Do you want to know what I think the best thing for you to do?"

I give her a sideways glance. "What?"

"Show him he's not the only guy you can get." She points at the crowd of guys a few feet away from us. "Look at all of them. If the jackass doesn't claim you publicly, show him he has no claim over you, period. Make him aware that you'll do whatever you want until he pulls his head out of his ass and mans up."

"That's the thing, though. He's never going to pull his head out of his ass because he doesn't want a commitment."

"Then that's another issue. Do you know what the only solution to the problem when a man who's afraid to commit is?"

I look at her but don't answer.

"Moving on. Forget about him. You might love him now, but you don't have to always love him. You're not Whitney Houston."

That's easier said than done. I've been in love with Bracken for so long I'm not sure I can move on without hating him.

seventeen

BRACKEN

"WHO'S THE LUCKY LADY?" the woman behind the counter asks. Her red fingernails slides open another glass showcase filled with sparkling diamonds and gold necklaces.

I went to high school with her, but I can't remember her name. I honestly don't give a shit what it is either. The only reason she's asking for details is so she can run off and tell her friends. That's the last damn thing I need getting back to Simon. I already have Nautica pissed off at me. I need to make shit right one person at a time.

"Someone special," is all I answer, with a shrug.

"Do I know her?" she pushes.

"Nope."

I look down at the thin, gold chain wrapped around my fingers. I've been in this jewelry store for almost an hour trying to find the perfect Christmas present for Nautica. I want to get her something she'll love, but I've never bought jewelry for a chick—other than my mom. I decided to go with a necklace after this no-name woman asked me if I was positive I didn't want to go with a ring fifteen times.

I haven't talked to Nautica since the whole ice-skating

disaster. I acted like an idiot. She put me on the spot, drilling me with questions I wasn't prepared to answer, so I stuck my foot in my mouth. My silence told her we're only fuck buddies, and that's it. I've never been good with words.

"Can I get this engraved?" I ask.

"Sure," she answers with a smile. "It may take a few days, but we can get it done for you."

"By Christmas?"

"By Christmas," she verifies with a nod.

I set the necklace down and pull out my wallet. "Sold."

* * *

Me: Do you have a minute to talk?

My phone beeps with a response.

Nautica: Nope.

Fuck. She's still pissed, but I got a response. That gives me some hope. I was worried I wouldn't even get that. An answer is something I can work with.

Me: Please. I'm sorry. Let me explain myself. Fix this.

Nautica: Fine. I'm at home. You can come over.

Me: To your house?

Nautica: Yes. Is that a problem?

She's testing me to see if I'm okay with possibly having to face Simon. I'm not about to fail.

I start to type out, *"Is Simon there?"* but backspace. That will only piss her off more. I retype.

Me: I'll be there in ten.

A sense of relief hits me when I pull up to see the driveway clear of Simon's car. I tuck the necklace receipt into my glove compartment and get out. The front door is unlocked, and I walk into the quiet house.

"Asshole." I look up to see a full-of-attitude Macy shaking

her head and stomping down the stairs with a grimace on her face. Her purse and keys are in her hand.

"It's a pleasure seeing you, too," I reply.

She snorts and shoves past me. "She's upstairs. You better get up there and say the right thing, or she's pretty much done with you." She smacks my shoulder on her way out the door.

"Great," I mutter. I head upstairs and knock on Nautica's bedroom door before opening it. She's lying on her stomach in bed and watching TV. She glances over and frowns when she sees me.

I lean back against the wall and shove my hands into my pockets. "Hey," I say.

"Hi," she replies softly. Her tangled hair is pulled away from her face and in a messy ponytail. She's wearing sweats and a T-shirt. Even dressed down like she doesn't give a care in the world, she still looks breathtaking. "You wanted to talk?"

I push myself off the wall. "I do, but I want to apologize first." I sit down on the edge of her bed. "I'm a dumbass. I messed up. The situation we're in is complicated, but that's not an excuse for me to act like a jackass. I don't want to hide anymore, and I don't want you to think of yourself as a secret. I'm going to talk to Simon about us."

She lifts up from her stomach and looks at me in shock. "Don't bullshit me, Bracken Casey."

I hold up my hands in surrender. "No bullshitting, I swear. I'm going to tell him before we head back to school. I plan on taking him out and breaking the news. He deserves to know. We deserve not to be sneaking around. I'll explain that we've hung out a few times and clicked. I'm going to leave out the part where we've started fucking, and that we still are—for obvious reasons."

She nods in agreement. I get excited when I notice the bright smile on her face. "Although, I'm sure he'll figure that out sooner or later. My brother isn't an idiot." Her grin grows wider. "Do you promise?"

I lean forward and twirl a loose strand of her hair around my finger. "I promise. I'll make this right."

I've never done commitment, but if I'm going to try it, it might as well be with someone I really care about, whose company I enjoy, and who is amazing in bed. If commitment is what she wants for me to keep having her, I'll try my best to give it to her.

She leans forward, grabs my head, and kisses me. "Thank you."

"Do I get a reward for my efforts?" I ask against her lips.

"Mm, I think that can be arranged." I bite into her lip as she grips my cock through my jeans. "What did you have in mind?"

I run my hands down her back and grab a handful of her ass. *Fuck, her ass is perfect.* "I'm sure whatever you give me is going to be amazing, baby."

"I like that answer."

"Probably not as much as I'm going to like the reward."

My dick springs out from my jeans. She wastes no time before wrapping her slick, thick lips around it. I grip her hair to control her pace. It feels so good, but I can't lose my shit yet. I need to fuck her.

"Bend over," I say, panting.

She looks up at me with her mouth still full of my cock.

"Quit sucking my dick, take off your panties, and bend over for me."

I hiss when she releases my dick. I glance down at my throbbing erection as she pushes herself off the bed and stands up. My eyes stay glued to her every move. She slowly strips off her shirt and tosses it on the floor with a girlish smile.

"Keep going," I say. I wrap my fist around my cock and start to pump up and down. "Don't stop."

Her bra is the next to go. She slides each strap off her shoulders before unclasping it and letting it fall to the floor. I lick my lips, my mouth salivating as I eye her hard nipples.

"You wanted me to bend over?" she asks innocently. She twirls a dark strand of hair around her finger playfully. "Why, Bracken, do you want me to bend over for you?"

"You know why," I grunt. My hand is moving faster on my cock. "I'm not in the mood to play games."

"What are you in the mood for?"

"To fuck you." My answer comes out sounding like a growl.

I jump up from the bed, wrap my arms around her waist, and push her against the front of her desk. I rub my hard cock along her ass. She doesn't fight me as I tug down her pants, along with her panties. She lets out a moan, her ass pushing against me, when I plunge into her.

"Oh god, yes," she cries out.

"This is exactly what I was in the mood for," I whisper into her ear.

She shivers as I drop soft kisses along the nape of her neck.

"This is what I'm always in the mood for."

Her head falls back along my shoulder, and I brush my lips against hers before sliding my tongue in her mouth. "Don't stop," she begs, meeting my pace. Her hips slam back against me with every thrust.

I inch my hand up her chest, playing with her tits.

"God ... I'm close."

"Me too. Fuck, your pussy feels so good."

"What the fuck is going on here?"

She jumps forward. I jump back. My dick slides out of her. *Fuck, this isn't good.* I grab a blanket from the bed and throw it over her naked body before turning around and facing him— my dick still in its full glory.

Oh shit.

Simon is standing in the doorway with his legs planted wide, his arms crossed, and his nostrils flaring. I can hear his breathing from across the room. This isn't how I wanted it to go down.

I grab my pants from the bed and battle with myself on what the next words that come out of my mouth are going to be as I pull them on. Whatever I come up with better be good. It also needs to be smart enough that he doesn't hate my ass or try to kill me.

"It's not what it looks like," sounds like a good option, but it also sounds like a stupid as fuck response. I'm so fucked.

"Simon! Get out!" Nautica yells. She wraps the blanket tighter around her and sits down on the edge of the bed.

He puts his hand up, stopping her. "Don't you fucking say a word."

"We need to talk. Let's go to the other room," I finally say, my voice cool and controlled.

"You're damn straight we need to," he says. He charges toward me. "You're my best friend. The only guy I've ever trusted with her, and you do this? You were like my brother, man." His tone is a mixture of anger and hurt, which makes me feel even more like an asshole.

His fist is hard against my cheek. I allow him one punch.

Just one.

I deserve it. My head flies back against the wall, and I gain control of myself before he tries to throw another one. He stumbles back when my palms connect with his chest.

"Calm your ass down, Simon!" I yell.

Nautica frantically gets dressed underneath the blanket. "Simon, don't be mad at him," she begs. "It's both of our faults."

He spins around and points at her. "You shut the fuck up. I'll deal with you later."

"Dude, don't talk to her like that," I warn. "You can be

pissed off at me all you fucking want, but don't take it out on her."

Nautica doesn't deserve this shit. If he wants to punch someone, if he wants to cuss someone out, he should pick me.

"Don't tell me how to talk to my damn sister," he spats, spit flying from his lips. "Get the hell out of my house. You stay the fuck away from her, or I will kill you."

"I'm in love with him," Nautica blurts out.

I stumble back against the wall. *Oh fuck.* This is definitely the wrong time to start making love devotions. I'm trying to keep my ass from getting kicked.

Simon laughs mockingly. "That's sweet, little sister, but you can't honestly believe he feels the same way." He swings around to look directly at her. "This bastard doesn't *love* anyone but himself. He's using you, just like he does with every other girl he's fucked. And trust me, there's been a shit ton of them." He turns to look back at me. "Which is exactly why I told you to stay the fuck away from her!"

I drag a hand through my hair and pull at the ends. "I tried. I really did, but it was impossible."

I have feelings for her. I want to tell him that, but now isn't the time, especially after she just said the four-letter word. I can't compete with that, so I'm not going to try.

I don't see it coming until his fist connects with my jaw again. I shuffle back into the wall, knocking down a few pictures and a chair. *Damn, he knows how to catch a man off guard.*

"I deserved that." I wipe the blood off my lip. "I'll let you have those two, but that's it."

He takes another swing, but I move too quickly, and his fist goes through the wall behind me.

"Motherfucker!" he grunts, and inspects his now bloody fist.

We are dripping blood on the carpet. Their mom is going to have a fit.

"Simon, stop!" Nautica jumps up from the bed. She rushes over and tries to grab him but goes stumbling back when his arm flies out and accidentally hits her in the stomach.

I shoot toward them and push him out of the way to help her up. "You need to calm the fuck down," I yell, easing her down on the bed. I shift around to look at him, creating a wall between her and him.

He spits at my feet. "Fuck you. Get the hell out of my house."

"I will when you calm your ass down and talk to me."

I've never seen him like this. I knew the reaction I'd get from him when he found out wouldn't be pretty, but I didn't think it'd be *this* bad.

"Fuck you," he repeats. "Fuck the both of you. I'm out."

He storms out of her bedroom, pushing away everything in his path, and stomps down the stairs. Nautica falls down on her back at the same time the front door slams shut.

"That definitely didn't go as planned," she says, hugging herself. She covers her face, trying to hide the tears streaming down her cheeks.

I grab a tissue and hold it against my nose to capture the blood. "Don't cry," I say, sitting down next to her and carefully prying her hand away. I start to wipe away the tears. "He'll cool off. I'll talk to him. I'll fix this." I'm trying to convince myself just as much as I am her that Simon will eventually forgive us. "He's in shock right now. He'll take a drive, clear his head, and we'll talk shit out."

She nods. "You're right."

I pull her into my side and kiss her forehead. "Everything will be fine."

* * *

My head is pounding.

I'm lying in bed next to Nautica, my arms wrapped around her, as my mind goes through everything I did wrong. Everything I could've changed. I should've told him sooner. I shouldn't have hidden it from him. Now, I have to figure out how to fix this disaster I created.

I untangle myself from her at the sound of her phone and grab it from the nightstand. "It's your mom," I say, handing it to her.

Did Simon tell her about what he walked in on? Does she hate me now, too? He's been gone for almost thirty minutes now. I'm not leaving until he comes back and we work this shit out.

She grabs the phone and answers it. I make myself comfortable but keep my eyes on her when I notice all her muscles tense up. Her mouth falls open as a strangled cry escapes her lips. Her hand goes to her throat as tears start to flow. Something isn't right, and it's something worse than Simon being mad at us.

"Babe, what is it?" I ask.

She only shakes her head in response. "Where is he now?" she questions into the phone, choking back a sob. "What are they saying?" She nods a few times, listening to her mom.

"What's going on?" I ask again, my voice cracking.

"Simon," she says. "He's at the hospital. He got into a car accident, and he's in critical condition."

My stomach drops as fear charts through me. "Let's go."

This changes everything.

eighteen

NAUTICA

"YOU'RE BEING QUIET," I whisper, panic rising with every passing breath. I don't know what's going on with Simon. I don't know what's going on with Bracken. I don't know what's going on with anything anymore.

Bracken is speeding toward the hospital, and I'm worried we're going to end up in the room next to Simon if he doesn't slow down. He hasn't said a word since we threw on our coats, rushed out of the house, and got into his truck.

We make it to the parking lot in half the normal time, and he swerves into the first open spot.

"I'm not in the mood to talk," he says roughly. His knuckles pale as he grips the steering wheel. "Have you heard anything else from your mom?"

I shake my head. "She told me to go through the emergency entrance, and she'll be in the waiting room," I reply, reciting the words of her last text.

"Then let's go." He jumps out at the same time the door swings open and heads toward the entrance without waiting for me. *What the fuck?* I have to pick up my pace to keep up with him.

My mom runs straight into my arms when she sees me. Tears, along with streams of mascara, are running down her face. "They said they're not sure if he's going to make it," she cries out. Sobs pour from her. "He hasn't woken up." More sobs, harder this time. "I can't lose him!"

I tighten my arms around her as I try to control my own emotions but am doing a horrible job at it.

"I can't lose my son," she mutters. "I've already lost one man I loved. I can't do it again."

My heart aches as she pulls away and falls down in a chair. I sit down next to her and grab her hand in mine. "Everything is going to be okay," I tell her. "Simon will get through this. He's strong." I hope I sound more assured than I feel.

I look over at Bracken. His face is white as he looks back and forth between the door and us.

"I've ... I've got to get the hell out of here," he says, backing away.

"What?" I ask, jumping up from my chair. "Where are you going?"

He turns his back to me and races to the doors. "I have to get the fuck out of here."

I kiss my mom's cheek before rushing after him. I don't catch up until we're almost to his truck. "You have to get out of here?" I ask. "Why?" I dart forward and tug on the sleeve of his coat, trying to stop him with all my strength. I lose my hold when he whips around to face me.

"Fucking stop, Nautica," he yells. "Just let me go." He points at the hospital. "This is all our fault. *My* fault. I should've stayed the hell away from you. I was an idiot who couldn't control his dick. This would've never happened if I didn't touch you. Your mom wouldn't be sitting in the emergency room unsure if her son is going to die."

"No," I say, shaking my head violently. His words hit me like a train, making me feel light-headed. "That's not true, and you know it."

"He could be dead in there, and the last thing that was on his mind, the last thing he saw, was *us*. Us betraying him. I can't ..." He walks backward. "I can't do this anymore. It's wrong. It's ... we're over."

I flinch. "What? You think this is what he'd want?" I scream, ignoring the curious looks from a couple taking a smoke break a few feet away. "Do you think he'd want you to leave me alone like this? At this time? You have to be there for him, too."

"I think he'd want me to stay away from you, which is exactly what I'm going to do."

I charge forward, and he stumbles back when I push on his chest. "You're such a fucking coward, you know that? Go ahead. Run away. Run away because it's convenient and you don't want to deal with real-life consequences." I push him again. "Simon was right." My voice turns ice cold. "You were only using me. All you care about is getting laid. I hate you."

"This has nothing to do with me! This is about you, not hurting you, not hurting Simon, or your mom. None of this is me being selfish. If I stay with you, that would be selfish!"

"Bullshit. If you want to believe that lie to sleep better at night, go right ahead. But we both know it's a goddamn cop-out." I race forward to push him again. "Go."

He stumbles back.

"Leave me, Bracken. Show me how much you care about me."

And that's exactly what he does. He pulls away and walks to his truck. I collapse onto the dirty, snow-covered ground and cry as the loud motor starts up, and he speeds out of the parking lot.

nineteen

BRACKEN

HEARING her cries and witnessing her sobs tears me apart as I walk away, but I'm doing the right thing, even if it kills me with every step.

She doesn't understand. She thinks I'm being weak and running away, but that's not it. This is a sign we're not meant to be. I thought that it could work, that I could be the man she wants me to be, but it's impossible.

Damn straight I have feelings for her. I can't deny that shit, but I'm not sure if it's love because I don't know what the fuck love is. I've never witnessed anything but fake love and feelings my entire life.

On the outside, my parents have the picture-perfect, sunshine marriage. My father owns the dealership and supports the family while my mom is the homemaker.

But on the inside, it's darker. There is no happiness. No love. Only emptiness. My mom pops Xanax like it's candy. My father has a drinking and I'm pretty positive a monogamy problem. To be honest, they can't stand each other. She resents him for asking her to quit her dreams of teaching. He resents her for not being the perfect wife. He sees it in black and white.

He handed her the American dream on a silver platter: the nice house, the manicured lawn, and the walls of secrets and unhappiness.

I don't want to be like my father, but I know it's inevitable. I know I'll be the man who pays too much attention to his job and not enough to his wife. I'm stepping away now before I ruin her, before she chooses me over her family, and has no one to turn to after I destroy her.

If it came down to Simon or me, she'd choose me. Something about love makes you cut the wire to anyone who isn't rooting for you. I can't do that to her, especially when I'm not sure if I'll always be there to lift her up.

I told Nautica I was ready for a commitment, and everything blew up in our faces. My mom told me years ago that commitment is for fools. It brings out the true flaws and demons in people. The fights about money, about who works more hours, and who has to change all the shitty diapers rips you apart. That spark that once shined so bright will fizzle out more and more after every argument, every cruel word said to each other, and eventually, you'll be left in the dark.

And on top of it all, I'll never forgive myself if Simon doesn't make it. He left angry and was probably speeding. That would've never happened if he hadn't walked in on me fucking his sister.

I had to leave before I lost it. I couldn't look at her or her mom any longer. They already lost one man they loved. Adding Simon to that list will kill them.

* * *

I drive around until it's dark outside and visiting hours are almost over before heading back to the hospital. I kill the engine and pray that Nautica has already left. I know the chances of her being here are high, but I have to see him. I have to know if my best friend is going to live or not.

I make it through the front door and into the waiting room, but stop when I see it.

When I see *them*.

The funny thing about people trying to hide secrets is that it seems like a spotlight is always on them. As hard as you try to be sneaky, your lies make you stand out.

My blood boils as I watch Pamela and my father in the waiting room. She's wrapped in his arms and sobbing. He pulls away and wipes the tears from her red cheeks.

The way he's whispering in her ear, and how she's holding him for dear life tells me everything I need to know.

That motherfucking asshole.

I turn around and sprint back out to my car before I do something stupid.

Then I wait.

Thirty minutes pass. I perk up when I spot them leaving. His arm is slumped over her shoulders as he guides her toward her SUV. He opens up the car door and kisses her on the cheek before she slides in.

As soon as she pulls away, I jump out of my truck and stalk toward him.

"What the fuck is going on with you and Pam?" I shout.

His body goes solid before he turns around to face me. He looks around the deserted parking lot. "This is not the place, son," he answers calmly.

"Answer my damn question."

"Let's go talk in my truck."

I lunge forward and snatch him up by his collar. "You piece of shit. You've been fucking around on Mom with her?"

He pushes me away to break out of my hold. "Oh, come on, Bracken. You had to know. Your mom ... she's not herself anymore. I don't even know who the hell she is. I've already filed for divorce, we both have attorneys, and I'm being very fair to her. I'm giving her half of everything and the lake house, so she'll be happy."

I scoff. "Oh, you're trying to buy her off for cheating on her?" I shove my finger in his face. "You're a piece of shit. You could've at least waited until you signed the papers before jumping into bed with another woman."

He shakes his head. "Please, let's go talk somewhere."

"I have nothing else to say to you." I spit at his feet and walk away.

In one day, I lost both of my best friends. All because of sex.

twenty

NAUTICA

"DO you want some company in there?" Macy asks, parking in my driveway.

I'm not sure how late it is, or how long I'd been at the hospital. All I know is it's dark outside, and my heart is breaking more and more the blacker the sky gets.

"No," I answer, gripping the door handle. "I'm exhausted. I want to collapse in my bed and sleep off this nightmare."

Macy showed up at the hospital with tears in her eyes as soon as she got the call from me. We sat in the waiting room with my mom, desperate for updates, but those were minimal. Simon is still in critical condition. The doctor said all we can do now is play the waiting game to see if he worsens or improves.

Fear and resentment eat at me. The two men I love the most turned their backs on me today, and I'm not sure if they're ever coming back.

She stares out the windshield and nods. "I'll keep my phone on in case you or your mom need anything," she says. "Call me if you get any updates. I don't care what time it is." A few tears trickle down her cheek. "I still can't believe this happened."

I wipe away my own tears. "I'll call you as soon as I hear something."

I pull on the handle and get out. I head inside and check my phone on the way upstairs, hoping to see my mom's or Bracken's name.

Nothing.

I don't know when my mom is coming home, or if she even is. Randy stopped by the hospital an hour ago to check on us and offered to stay with her so I could get some rest. When I asked if he'd talked to Bracken, he only shook his head.

I strip off my clothes and get in bed. I dial Bracken's number, but it goes to voicemail—the same it has all day. I send him a text asking him to call me and set my phone next to my pillow.

twenty-one

NAUTICA

I THROW my phone down onto the kitchen counter. "I'm going to kill him," I say around a groan.

It's been six days of calling Bracken, and six days of getting his voicemail. They say that being ignored causes the same chemical reaction in the brain as physically being hurt does. I believe it. I feel like I'm getting stabbed with a double-edged dagger with every, *"You have reached the voicemail of..."*

Yesterday was Christmas. My mom and I spent all day at the hospital. They transferred Simon from ICU and into his own room. He's no longer in critical condition and is making progress. He's no longer on the respirator and is breathing on his own. The doctors say his improvement is remarkable, and the outlook is promising. Simon is a fighter. He'll be home with us soon.

"Give him time, honey," my mom responds. She pours a glass of orange juice and hands it to me.

She's repeated that same advice to me every day since Simon's accident and Bracken leaving me. The other night, she broke down and told me about her affair with Randy. She explained how Bracken saw them at the hospital and blew up on his dad. According to Randy, he stormed off, went home, packed his bags, and left with his mom. No one has heard from him since, but his mom did send a text telling Randy they are both okay.

They were waiting for Randy's divorce to be finalized before telling us. I know it's wrong to break up a marriage, but deep down, I understand in a weird way. My mom was fighting the pull she had toward someone she couldn't have. I can't look down on her because I've felt the same way. I'm happy the man she loves at least reciprocates the feelings. She deserves to be happy.

"Give him time?" I repeat with a scoff. "I've given him almost a week. I don't understand why he won't pick up the phone or even send me a damn text to let me know he's okay and not in some ditch dead somewhere."

She gives me an emphatic look. "Try to see where he's coming from. Bracken is probably blaming himself for Simon's accident because he left upset with you two. He thinks keeping his distance from you will make Simon happy. He's scared to face reality, not sure if he'll ever be forgiven. When Simon gets better, he'll reach out to him, let him know everything is okay, and Bracken will come back around. He just needs time."

I don't want to give him time. I need him back. My body aches at the thought of never seeing him again.

"But what about me? Why doesn't he care about how he's hurting me? Selfish bastard."

She rests her elbows on the counter. "The ones we love can be selfish at times. You need to decide if he's worth waiting for."

I shake my head. "You can't have a relationship with a selfish asshole. It's not possible because the second it gets rough, they're out the door, which is exactly what happened."

She opens her mouth to give me some more words of

wisdom, but the sound of the doorbell ringing stops her. I take the time she goes to answer it to pity myself.

"Were you expecting a package?" she asks, resurfacing with a box in her hands.

I think back to everything I've ordered for the holidays. "No."

She double-checks the name. "It's for you."

She hands me the box and opens up the drawer for a pair of scissors. There's no sender information. I cut it open and find a small box wrapped in red tissue paper. I look at her. She shrugs.

It's a jewelry box. *Who the hell sent me jewelry?*

There's a card. I grab it, and my stomach cramps as I start to read it.

Nautica,

I'm sorry for everything. I'll always remember us. I want you to be happy.

Merry Christmas,
Bracken.

I hold in a breath and grab the blue velvet box, playing with it in my hand. My eyes go wide as I pop open the lid. I pull out the necklace. The gold chain shimmers underneath the lights. A heart pendant with white and pink diamonds hangs from it. I hold it up, admiring its beauty from every angle, and catch sight of the words engraved on the back of the heart.

This is step one.

Step one?

This only magnifies my confusion. Of course, Bracken would lead me down a dead end like this.

"Wow, that's beautiful," my mom says in the distance.

I only nod because I'm incapable of forming words at this point. *Why would he send this to me? Does he want to keep torturing me?*

I carefully place the necklace back into the box and grab my phone. He doesn't answer my call.

Or the next one.

Or any of my texts.

When I go to bed, I fall asleep with my phone in my hand, but the call never comes.

I'm waiting on something that's never going to happen.

twenty-two

NAUTICA

"CAN I BORROW YOUR CAR?" I ask.

"To go where?" Macy replies. She zips up her bag and slides it underneath her bed.

We got back to school an hour ago, and I just finished unpacking. It's been eight days since Simon's accident. I offered to take off the semester to help my mom, but she said no. He broke his ribs and a leg in the accident and is unable to go back to base until he recovers. Telling him he couldn't go back to work for his tour is what he took the hardest.

He's apologized to me and tried calling Bracken a few times to do the same, but he gets the same thing I do: his voicemail.

It's like his phone has been permanently shut off. I even tried calling his mom, but she didn't answer either. The good thing is I know where to find him now. There's no way he's not coming back to school for his final semester.

I grab my coat and slide my phone into my pocket. "To Bracken's," I answer.

She clicks her tongue against the roof of her mouth. "Uh, are you sure that's a good idea?" Bracken is still on Macy's shit list, and she wants me to have nothing to do with him.

"Probably not, but I need to talk to him."

Uneasiness lines her features. "Do you want me to come with you?"

I shake my head. I need to do this alone.

She tosses me her keys. "Sure, but don't be fucking him in my back seat if you two make up."

"I can only hope it goes that well," I whisper under my breath.

I wave goodbye before scurrying out of my dorm. I trek through the snow-covered parking lot and get into her car. I keep it silent on the ride over while mentally going over everything I want to say to him. I fight with myself on whether to turn around and go back so many times I lose count.

My stomach tightens when I spot his truck in the parking lot, but there's also relief. *This is it.* I'm going to march in there and fix this. I take slow steps to his apartment. Jasper answers the door after a few knocks. His face drops when he sees me.

Not a good sign.

"Is Bracken here?" I ask, shivering as I tighten my scarf around my neck.

He lets out a sigh and looks over my shoulder in hesitation. "Uh ... he's ..."

I slap his shoulder, getting him to finally look at me. "Answer me," I order with a cold stare. It's fucking freezing, and my broken heart isn't in the mood for games.

"No. He went out for a little. I'll let him know you stopped by."

I point at his truck. "Weird, his truck is right there."

He scratches his head. "He ... uh ... drove my car."

"Liar," I grumble, pushing the door open wider and shoving past him.

Bracken never drives anything but his truck. I ignore Jasper's protests as I head straight toward Bracken's bedroom.

The door is shut. I don't bother knocking before barging in. Adrenaline is pumping through me like crazy.

What am I going to say to him? Is he still upset about everything?

Jasper is on my heels, still begging me to stop, and I stumble back into him when I take in the scene in front of me.

No. No.

I'm afraid I'm close to passing out as I give him all my weight. *This is a dream. Please be a dream.*

Jasper helps me back to my feet as I keep my eyes on Bracken. He's sitting on the edge of his bed, registered worry on his face, and he looks like he's seen a ghost. My gaze moves to the redhead next to him. Her eyes and face are red from crying, her hands are shaking, but that's not the worst part. In her hand is a pregnancy test.

I can feel my lunch ready to come up.

"Nautica," Bracken yells, causing me to jump. "You shouldn't have come here."

He snaps up from the bed and comes my way. His upper lip snarls like he has a reason to be pissed at me. Jasper moves out of our way and stands to the side, silently watching the shit show that is about to start.

"Actually, I should have." I shove his chest and fight back my own tears. "Guilt has been eating me alive, tearing me apart for everything that happened with us." It's getting harder to hold back my tears. "I thought maybe, just maybe, you were missing me as much as I was you. But obviously not, considering you have a chick in your bedroom holding a goddamn pregnancy test."

"You need to leave." He grabs my hand and starts to pull me through the hallway toward the front door.

I jerk out of his hold. "Thank you," I spat.

He stays quiet and doesn't look at me.

"Thank you for making me realize you're not worth the tears or the heartache. Fuck you, Bracken, and goodbye."

He stands there, hands in his pockets, and stares at the floor. He can't even look at me. I turn around and sprint out the door to the parking lot.

Jasper is the one who runs after me. Not Bracken. Not the man I'm in love with, and the one who just smashed my heart into a million pieces. He pounds on the car window until I roll it down.

"Nautica," he yells, out of breath. "Give him time … let him explain."

"You tell him he has a week, Jasper," I say. "One week, and then it's over. I'm done."

One week passes without word from him.

Two weeks pass.

Weeks turn into months.

Months turn into years.

twenty-three

NAUTICA

Five Years Later

THE CASKET IS black with gold trim.

I went to the funeral home with my mom three days ago to assist her in picking it out along with the other arrangements because she couldn't do it herself. My heart aches for her. It was the second time she was making funeral arrangements for someone she loved in a far too-little time span.

A heart attack.

No one saw it coming.

Randy had been working late after the dealership closed. My mom went to check on him when he didn't show up for dinner and wasn't answering his phone. It was too late when she found him in his office. He was gone before she even had the chance to call for help.

I cross my legs and focus on the casket. Photos of Randy with my mom, Bracken, and even his ex-wife are delicately placed along the lid and surrounded by an array of colorful floral arrangements.

I stare at one in particular of him and Bracken. It had to have been his freshman year and after a football game. Bracken is wearing his jersey as sweat glistens his forehead. A proud smile beams across Randy's face while he sports a T-shirt with his son's jersey number.

"Bracken," my mom whispers.

My gaze snaps from the photos to her. *What?* My mouth drops open when she stumbles out of her chair and straight into the strong arms of a man.

My heart thumps against my chest. I do a double take, praying I'm seeing things, and grip the arm of my chair for support.

Him.

I didn't expect him to show. Shit, no one expected him to show. After he let me walk away from him at his apartment, I thought I'd never see him again. He hasn't been in contact with anyone, including Randy. It's like he dropped us all and didn't give a shit about it.

I've been working on moving on from that part of my life. Now, five long and hard years later, the sight of him feels like a chainsaw straight through my heart.

"I'm so happy you came, honey," my mom says, her voice broken up in sobs. "Thank you." Her cries grow louder, drawing more attention our way. "Thank you so much."

The crowd starts to merge our way.

Just fucking great.

Back to the Bracken show.

My gaze pins to him, watching his every move. He pats her on the back while I hold in the urge to shoot up from my chair and punch him.

"You know I wouldn't miss this, Pam," he says calmly. He clutches her tighter in his hold before glancing over her shoulder, straight at me. His face is pale, his baby blue eyes swollen, and it looks like he hasn't slept in days. "I can't believe this happened." He shuts his eyes. "This isn't right."

It kills me to watch my mom crumple in the arms of the man I once loved. I still love. He holds her tight, soothing her with his entrancing voice that used to take me over. That voice still haunts me, giving me nothing but nightmares and tears.

His eyes slowly open, and he tries to gain eye contact with me, but I look away. He isn't getting shit from me unless it's to tell him to go to hell. I bite my tongue, nearly drawing blood. This is about my mom. I need to put my anger for him aside in support for her. I lean back in my chair, acting like I don't notice his presence.

He's ignored my existence for years. I owe him the same.

I look down the row at Simon sitting on the opposite side of my mom with his family. His mouth is drawn into a straight line as he rubs his clenched jaw. He's just as uneasy about Bracken being here as I am. I swear I notice Macy snarl at him.

He takes the open seat next to me when the service starts. I flinch, my mouth going dry, when he takes my hand in his. I'm itching to pull away and tell him not to touch me, but I can't. I don't want to look like a woman being rude to a grieving son. So, I slump deeper into my seat. The heat of his hand grows warmer as the service goes on. Tears fall down my cheeks, mourning the death of not only his father but also the memories of us.

I sneak a glance at him, and for the first time ever, I witness him cry.

We had something once.

Something that should've never happened.

Something that ripped through our lives like a tornado leaving no one unscarred.

He won't be here long. Won't stay.

History will repeat itself.

He's not getting close enough to break my heart this time.

twenty-four

NAUTICA

HE'S HERE in the flesh, standing in the living room, and acting like he never left us. The wound of him has painfully ripped back open.

I lean against the wall, my temper growing higher each time he greets someone walking through the front door. He steps to my mom's side anytime it looks like she's on the verge of another breakdown, acting like he's been a constant here.

My throat itches. I want to scream, make a scene, and tell him he doesn't belong here, but at the same time, I crave for him to wrap his arms around me. Even after all this time, the asshole still has power over me—making me feel things I don't want to. I hate him for that.

He looks good. Too damn good. His black suit fits him like it was perfectly tailored to his broad chest. His gold watch glistens underneath the light. His dark hair is swept back, giving me a view of his baby blues. A trimmed mustache runs along his upper lip as a short, kept beard covers the bottom of his face and strong chin. I've never been much of a beard girl ... but damn, I guess I just had to see it on the right man.

His arms are more defined, more muscular, and so are his

shoulders. Gone is the college boy I loved, replaced with this powerful, enthralling man with one arm covered in a sleeve of tattoos. He's changed so much. It feels like I know nothing about him.

Unable to watch him any longer, I duck into the kitchen to get everything ready. We're holding the reception at Simon's house—well, our old house. He bought the place after my mom and Randy purchased a new five-bedroom home, and she moved out.

I frown when I feel him at my back, following me.

"You're wearing the necklace," he says, looking straight at it when I turn around.

I look down and want to slap myself. In the middle of my chest, over my white blouse and between the lapels of my unbuttoned blazer, sits the necklace he sent me.

I forgot to take it off on the ride over here. I didn't want him to notice it. I wrap my fingers around the heart pendant and mindlessly play with it.

"It looks more beautiful on you than I imagined," he adds, running a hand through his beard.

I'm not sure *why* I put the damn thing on this morning. I haven't worn it in years. I threw it in the back of my jewelry box when the realization that he was never coming back finally sank in. For some reason, I took it out today, but I'm not going back and forth about what that reason is with him. I think it's a sign I need to sell it on eBay or something.

"I'm surprised you showed," I say. I can't hold back the nastiness in my tone.

He broke my heart, walked out on me, and didn't come back until tragedy came. Now, he's trying to act like nothing happened. He might be okay with pretending, but I'm not. I'm doing my best not to blow up on him because his father did just pass away. I can't kick a guy too hard while he's down—maybe just give him a little nudge.

"I'm surprised you thought I wouldn't," he replies.

I move around him and open the freezer. I took on the job of getting the reception arrangements together. Cooking isn't exactly one of my strong suits, so I ordered subs from a local sandwich shop, along with some chips and finger foods.

"You left everyone—practically fell off the face of the Earth. I honestly don't know what to expect from you anymore." I grab an ice tray, slam it down on the counter, and start to drag out the rest of the food. "How did you find out?"

I know it wasn't Simon or me, and I don't think my mom has his number.

He shoves his hands into the pockets of his black slacks. "My uncle called my mom."

"Good thing, because no one here knew how to get ahold of you."

"You don't think I regret that?" he asks sharply. "I never had a chance to apologize to my father or make our relationship better. I thought eventually enough time would pass that we could move on and make shit right, but it's too late now. He's gone, and I never told him how much I really loved him." His eyes squeeze shut as his voice lowers. "How much he meant to me."

I rub my cheek while avoiding all eye contact. "He loved you, and he knew you loved him."

"Yeah, but I had a pretty shitty way of showing it."

I won't argue with the truth, even if it will make him feel better.

"So, uh ... Simon and Macy?" He signals out to the living room, where my brother and best friend are sitting together.

"Yep."

Apparently, they had a little fling before we left for college and started it back up after Simon's accident. They married a few years ago.

That could've been us.

"And their daughter?"

I nod, thinking of my niece, Annabelle.

"Wow, she's almost a spitting image of you when you were younger."

I pop a pretzel in my mouth and scurry from behind the island to escape the kitchen. I have to get out of here. If we keep talking, I'm going to have a breakdown. I can't stay here and listen to him compliment me. I come to a halt when he grabs my arm. I shiver at the feel of his lips against my ear.

"Please don't run from me. We need to talk. I know this isn't the place to hash out our past and problems, but give me a chance to explain everything."

I yank out of his hold. "That's where you're wrong. We don't need to talk about anything. You're here. I know my mother appreciates it, but I don't need anything else from you. I don't care about an apology, an explanation, anything. That was years ago. I've moved on."

His face falls. "I came here for you, too," he says, his voice strained.

"It's too late." I resist the tingle in my hand to slap him across the face. "When this is over, you can go run back to where you came from." I can't look him in the eyes.

"Are you seeing someone?"

"We are *so* not doing this," I reply, flabbergasted. Is he really trying to ask me this *here?*

"Just tell me, *please*. Tell me."

"Leave me alone."

"This conversation, us talking shit out, will happen sooner or later."

"I'd prefer later ... or never."

I storm away from him and push through the crowd until I reach the stairs. I dart up to my old bedroom and slam the door shut behind me. Deep breaths pass through my lungs as I lean back against the door and curse to the air.

I had my worries about him showing up, but I tried to place them in the back of my mind. I tried to convince myself that he wouldn't come because Bracken couldn't man up and do the right thing. I guess I was wrong. I can't deal with that today, though. I have to be strong for my mom, even if Bracken is breaking me down.

I sit down on the floor. *Does he have a girlfriend? A wife?*

I'm pissed at myself for studying his hand and feeling a sense of relief when I noticed there was no sign of a wedding ring. He said he didn't do commitment. I guess he wasn't lying.

I look up at the knock on the door.

"Come in," I say hesitantly, hoping it's not Bracken on the other side.

Macy strolls in, gently shutting the door behind her. "He's here," she says, matter-of-factly.

"He's here," I repeat, running my hands over my face. Those two words mean so much.

"What are you going to do?"

"Stay as far away from him as I can." I get up and double-check my makeup in the vanity mirror. "He won't be here long. Hopefully, history will repeat itself, and he'll be gone." I unclasp the necklace and slip it into my pocket. "I have to get back downstairs to my mom."

Bracken is gone when we make it back down. Thank God, maybe my wish has been granted, and he's already skipped town.

twenty-five

BRACKEN

I WASN'T sure about the response I'd get when I walked into the funeral home, but I knew it wasn't going to be very welcoming. I couldn't blame them. I brought this upon myself.

I'm the one who created this turmoil and then hightailed it when it was time to deal with the consequences. I changed my number, cut off every tie linking me to this place, and haven't returned since.

When I got the call about my dad, it was like a sucker punch straight to the gut. My stubbornness had pulled me back, keeping me from making shit right with him before he passed. I hate myself for that. I would do anything to take it back.

And then there's her.

Nautica.

Every emotion, feeling, and memory I had with her came crashing into me like a Mack truck when I spotted her sitting there. She hates me. I knew it the moment she noticed me. Her dark eyes narrowed, her red lips grimaced, and her olive skin paled. She doesn't want anything to do with me.

I have to rectify that. It isn't going to be easy. I'm well aware I have making up to do. She's stubborn as hell, and I know it's going to take some time. It took me years to figure my own shit out. I owe her the same.

I glance up when I hear someone coming into the kitchen. I gulp when Pamela pulls out the chair next to me and has a seat. A tissue is clutched in her hand, and she's staring at me with glassy eyes.

"Bracken," she greets, letting out a sigh.

I nod in response, giving her a gentle smile. She's keeping it together well for a woman who's been widowed for the second time. It's obvious she's grieving, but she's doing better than what I imagined. I guess people really do build up more strength with each loss.

Her dark hair is wrapped up in a bun at the base of her neck, and her face is makeup-free, which I'm certain is because she was afraid of having it run down her face at the service. My mom did the same thing.

"Hi," I finally reply. "How are you dealing with all this?" My voice cracks at the end. *This.* I'm not even ready to say the word out loud ... *death.* He's gone.

She lets out a long breath. "As good as I can be, I guess." A small hint of a smile wavers along her thin lips. "Thank you for coming again. I really appreciate it. I was afraid the news wouldn't get to you in time."

"I owe you an apology. You. My dad. All of you deserve an apology. What I did was immature and wrong."

Her cold, shaking hand folds over mine. "Don't feel bad. I understand it was hard for you. You were put in a bad position. I forgive you." She squeezes my hand before removing hers. "Has Nautica talked to you yet?"

"If you count basically telling me to go screw myself, then yeah, a little bit."

She nods, not looking one bit surprised at her daughter's response. "It's going to be a hard job of getting back in her good graces. I don't know if you're staying here, leaving, or seeing someone, but if you want to make things right with her, you need to give her time. You hurt her. My daughter is not someone who forgets easily. You know her well enough to know she can't pretend you didn't leave her." She turns and points toward the living room. "The same thing with him, but I think he might be a little more easy-going with forgiveness. Trust me when I say there's nothing harder than trying to fix the woman's heart you broke *and* win her back."

I nod, playing with my phone in my pocket. "Do they all still have the same phone numbers?"

"All of us do. Make use of them."

I couldn't delete their numbers, even after I changed my own. Sometimes, I'd stare at their names on the screen and fight with myself on whether to hit delete or call. I never did either.

"How's your mom taking it?" she asks.

"She's doing okay." I hesitate for a moment. "She wasn't sure about showing up here because of ... everything." I invited my mom to come along, but she stayed behind. She didn't think she'd be welcome even though I tried to tell her differently.

"She's more than welcome to come here or my house anytime. She was a huge part of Randy's life, too."

A crowd shuffles into the kitchen, interrupting us to give their condolences. I kindly thank them before dashing out of the room and heading outside. I not only need fresh air but I also need to check on my mom and figure out a plan to make things right again.

I'm almost in the clear when the familiar voice stops me.

"Hey, wait up."

I turn around on my heels to see Simon coming my way.

"We need to talk," he says.

I point at my truck. "Get in."

twenty-six

NAUTICA

THE SCHOOL SUPERINTENDENT offered me as many bereavement days as I wanted, but I'm going back to work after only three. It will take my mind off things and clear my head from my never-ending thoughts of Bracken. He's been haunting me since he came back, and I need to stop letting myself wonder whether he's still in town.

I haven't seen or heard from him since the funeral. His mom showed up at Simon's a few hours after he left and ended up having a heart-to-heart with mine to clear the air.

I have a bagel in one hand, my briefcase in the other, and am on my way out of my apartment when someone knocks on the door. *What the ...?* No one stops by this early. I balance the strap of my bag on my shoulder and answer it.

"Holy shit, you really are a teacher."

I tighten my hold on the bagel and narrow my eyes at Bracken, who's standing in my doorway eyeing me up and down while he bites into the edge of his lip.

Well, there goes my day.

"I shouldn't be thinking the things I'm thinking right now,

but damn, fantasies of you in that skirt are going to be keeping me up at night," he goes on.

I take a good look at him. Beads of sweat are running along his forehead and neck. His white, sleeveless shirt shows off his tattoos. I wish I had more time to study each one and ask him about them. His hair is wet and messier than it had been at the funeral. Sweatpants hang loose on his hips.

Shit. Why does the man always have to look so damn good?

Him showing up at my front door out of the blue isn't what I need this morning.

I take a step back. "What the hell are you doing here?"

"Someone gave me your address." He shrugs. "I was on a run and thought it'd be cool to drop by and say hi."

Is he serious? *Drop by and say hi?* Like we're old friends? I plan on kicking whoever *that someone's* ass is. "I didn't ask how you got here. I asked what you're doing here."

I don't have the time or patience to play his games this early. I overslept, and I'm a week behind on papers to grade.

He leans into the doorframe. "I wanted to talk."

Bad timing, buddy. His answer infuriates me. *Now.* He wants to talk to me on *his* time. He's a day late and a dollar short if he thinks that's happening.

"I can't talk, Bracken. I have to go to work. I have shit to do, and hearing your excuses isn't on my agenda."

His face falls. Does he really think it's going to be that easy? That he can show up at my door, and I'll jump right back in his arms?

"Work ... yeah ... right." He blocks me from stepping around him. "What about later? Let's talk when you get off. I'll take you to dinner. I'll make you dinner. I'll do whatever you want."

"I have dinner plans."

"Where? With who?"

"That's actually none of your business."

I try to maneuver around him, but he slams his hand back against the doorframe, stopping me. "Don't do this. Don't act this way. I understand you're fucking pissed. I get it. But give me a chance."

"No, I'm beyond pissed. I want nothing to do with you, and that's your fault. So, leave me the hell alone. Nothing is going to change my mind about you." I duck underneath his arm to squeeze past him.

He moves out of the way as I shut my door and lock it.

"Now, I have to go to work. Don't show up here again."

I walk away from him and don't look back once. What he doesn't know is that my heart is pounding with every step, and I'm holding back tears. How can one man have such a tight control over my heart? And why can't I loosen the strings?

I dial Macy's number as soon as I get into my SUV.

"He showed up at my house this morning," I blurt out when she answers. "At my fucking house."

She gasps. "Shut the hell up." She doesn't even have to ask who *he* is.

"Did you give him my address?" My voice sounds more accusatory than it should, but my pulse is skyrocketing.

"Absolutely not. You know me. I hate that asshole for what he did to you."

"Then who?" *My mom?*

"Fucking Simon," we both say at the same time. My money is on him.

"That man, I don't understand him. He knows the shit Bracken put you through," Macy says.

"Years ago, he wanted to kill Bracken for touching me. Now, he's giving him my damn address? He needs to make up his mind."

She lowers her voice. "You know he regrets all that, don't you? He wishes he wouldn't have snapped like he did."

Simon's guilt from the day he walked in on us is strong. He punched his best friend, stormed out to his truck, and took off speeding. He ran a red light and t-boned another car with two passengers. They were all rushed to the hospital with Simon in the worst condition. Everyone made it out alive. When he woke up and everything became clear, he hated himself, and it took him some time to fight the demons of his guilt.

He's apologized countless times about blowing up on us, and I know losing Bracken hurt him, too. I feel guilt from that.

I start the engine and back out of the parking lot. "I know he does."

I don't blame Simon for Bracken leaving. Bracken is a big boy. He left on his own. When you love someone, you don't give a shit who's trying to push you away from them or tear you apart. You fight it. You fight for your love and happiness. I fought my part in the war and would've done anything for him. Bracken didn't, and I hate him for that.

"Are you still coming over for dinner?" she asks.

"Yeah. I have dance practice after school and then I'll be there."

"Can't wait to see you. Don't worry about him today, okay? Everything will work out."

"Everything will work out as soon as he's out of town and out of my mind."

twenty-seven

BRACKEN

I DIDN'T PLAN on stopping by Nautica's place this morning on my run.

Okay, shit. Maybe I did, but I'm trying to convince myself it was a spur-of-the-moment thing – just like all of the other shit that's happened between us. The sex, the feelings, the fallout, all of those things hadn't been anticipated, but they happened.

Our relationship has been full of thoughtless actions, no hesitations or worry about consequences.

I nearly lost my shit when she answered the door, looking all put together, prim and proper. The fucking a teacher fantasy has never been a turn-on for me ... until now. I can't stop thinking about marching into her classroom and bending her over the desk. She'll remember all the dirty things I did to her every time she sits there and grades papers.

She looks amazing, which isn't surprising. She's left her charcoal-colored hair long, but it now has a hint of blond high-lights to it. She was wearing it straight instead of curly, making her look older. She's all grown up. Her tits and ass are more filled out, making me feel more like the fucking idiot I am for walking away from her.

I'm stunned some other motherfucker hasn't scooped her up and put a ring on it. When I walked into the funeral home, I expected Quinton to be at her side, but there was no sign of him —thank fucking God. The asshole didn't show, giving me the perfect in. *Thank you, douchebag football player.*

I roll to a stop, put my truck in park, and take a deep breath before getting out and heading inside the small diner. I spot him sitting in a corner booth, and he waves me over.

"Well, well, look what the cat dragged in," he says, lifting up from his seat as I move his way.

"Hey, man," I say when I reach him. We give each other the whole man-hug clap thing on the back and sit down.

After Simon stopped me before leaving the reception, we talked briefly in my truck before he had to go back in to support Pam. He wasn't as pissed off to see me as Nautica was, but he hadn't been exactly jumping up and down either. I texted him and asked if he wanted to meet for lunch today. We need to clear the air.

Simon blows out a breath. "Wow ... didn't think this would happen anytime soon," he says. "But I'm glad it is. I'm happy we're sorting this shit out."

The biggest change since we last saw each other is his grown-out hair. He's still built, and age hasn't taken a toll on him yet. He looks the same age as the last time I saw him— when he was punching me in the face. He does have the fatherly thing going on, though. Instead of wanting to go out for beers, we're at a damn diner. I guess no more day drinking for him.

I give the waitress my order before answering him. "Me, too. This shit has been stretched out for far too long."

"How long?" he asks.

"Huh?" I stretch out my arm along the back of the booth, raising a brow.

"How long did you two have something going on?"

Fuck. I wasn't planning on giving him details of what went on between Nautica and me. I figured she'd already told him, or he didn't want to hear that shit.

"I don't think that's any of your business," I answer with a huff. "Not trying to be an asshole, but it's kind of personal. I'll only tell you it wasn't too long before you found out."

"Okay, I'll take that. Nautica is about as tight-lipped about it as you are. At least to me. I'm pretty sure Macy's little ass knows everything."

"Speaking of Macy ..." I hold back the urge to point out that he'd pretty much done the same thing as me. I'm sure he didn't ask Nautica to sign a permission slip for him to start fucking her best friend.

He slaps the table and chuckles. "I'm not going to deny it makes me look like a hypocritical asshole."

I don't bother correcting him.

"Do you remember the night you took Nautica to the holiday party?"

"Yeah," I croak out. How could I forget? My mind goes crazy —remembering how I bent her over the desk and pounded into her.

"Macy is the girl I hung out with."

"I knew you were hiding something, you sneaky bastard."

"I know ... I'm a dick. We ended up fucking the night before I left for the military." He runs his hand through his dark hair, unable to hold back the childish grin on his face. "I don't know how the hell it happened, but it did. When we both came back, she wanted to talk. We ended up doing that and a little bit more." He takes a sip of water. "She was there for me after the accident, and somehow, I ended up falling in love with her. She got pregnant four years ago with Annabelle, and we just celebrated our second anniversary."

"Wow," I say. Macy and Simon. I never thought I'd see the day. He did nothing but bitch about Nautica hanging out with her.

"It's shitty, I know, that I punched you over hiding the fact that you were with Nautica when I was fucking Macy on the side, but she's my *baby sister,* man. I was in shock. I never thought I had to worry about you doing that shit."

"Trust me, it wasn't planned. It just crept up on us, and we couldn't stop. I know I should've come to you, man to man. I was planning on it, I promise, but everything blew up before I had the chance to."

He nods in agreement. "So, now that we got that out of the way, do you forgive me?"

I chuckle. "For being an asshole, yes." I point my finger at him, trying to look more serious than I actually am. "For punching me? Do it again, and I'll have to beat your ass."

He throws his head back in laughter. "Yeah, I was pushing my limits. I was waiting for you to swing back so I could use it as more reason for Nautica to stay away from you."

"Prick."

"It's my baby sister. It took me a minute to realize she's grown." He laces his fingers behind his head. "So tell me what's your plan with her?"

"What do you mean?"

He scoffs, "Oh shut the fuck up. You asked me for her address. You haven't skipped town yet. I know you like my ass and all, but I'm sure I'm not the reason you're still here."

"I've been thinking about it," I mutter, taking a sip of coffee.

"Good luck with that. I'll help you, but it's probably not going to be easy."

"Trust me, I'm fucking figuring that out."

* * *

I stop at the doorway of my guest bedroom and notice her luggage is open on the bed. She has a stack of clothes sitting next to it.

"Are you going somewhere?" I ask.

My mom looks back at me, startled. "Yes, back home," she answers, picking up the clothes and carefully setting them in the suitcase. "My time here is done."

I hadn't expected her to stay long. She has a life and a job back home in Kansas, where she moved to be closer to me after the divorce.

I lean against the doorframe. "Do you want me to drive you?" I ask.

She waves her hand through the air. "No. George is on his way to pick me up."

As if on cue, the doorbell rings. I go to answer it and find George standing in front of me with a bouquet in his hand.

"Hey, Bracken," he says, walking in. "Thanks for taking care of my woman for me." He slaps me on the back as I lead him to my mom.

George is her husband as of a year ago. After I found out about my dad's affair, I went home and broke the news to my mom. The sad part is that she already knew. She'd gone through my dad's phone one day, saw their messages, and confronted him. He told her he was filing for divorce. That's why she'd been more distraught over the break. She was dealing with having a failed marriage and no one to turn to.

We ended up packing our shit and spending the rest of the holiday at a bed and breakfast a few hours out of town. She got an apartment with her spousal support, and I got a job to pay for my apartment until I graduated. I opened up a dealership with Jasper, and she started working for us. That's where she met our finance manager, George.

I give her a kiss on the cheek and tell them goodbye.
Now it's time to get my shit together.

twenty-eight

NAUTICA

IT'S after five o'clock when I pull up to Simon's house. It's been a long day but started to look up after I settled myself down from the whole Bracken showing up at my front door fiasco. A smile grew on my face when I'd walked into my classroom and found an array of flowers and cards from my students and other faculty members.

I'm in my first year of teaching at the same school I attended as a child, and I love it. I also coach the dance team.

My heels click against the driveway as I make my way to the front door. For the past year, Simon and Macy have had dinner at their house every Wednesday night. It's a nice way for us to catch up since we all have busy lives.

I walk into the living room but stop dead in my tracks as my breathing quickens. "What the hell are you doing here?" I ask, trying to keep my voice low in case Annabelle is around.

Is this some kind of setup?

I perch my hands on my hips, waiting for his explanation. He laughs at my cold glare, pissing me off more.

Bracken is sprawled out on the leather couch, looking like it's an everyday occurrence, with a beer in his hand. My brother looks over at me from the recliner in the corner. His eyes move to Bracken while we both wait for him to say something.

Bracken tips his beer my way with a grin. "I'm here for dinner, just like you."

"And who invited you?"

"I did, sis," Simon finally says.

I turn to glare at him, ignoring the arrogant smile on his face.

He snatches the remote from the table to turn down the volume on the TV. "We needed to catch up on some shit. Plus, I thought everyone would like to visit with him."

Everyone but me, apparently.

"You needed to catch up on some shit?" I repeat.

He nods.

"Can't you do that over the phone?"

He shakes his head. Bracken is smart and decides to stay quiet this time.

I roll my eyes and let out a long, exaggerated huff. I probably look childish as I storm out of the living room and into the kitchen, but I don't care. I'm pissed off and annoyed. I collapse onto a chair at the island and blow out a harsh breath.

"I take it you saw our additional dinner guest?" Macy asks, looking at me as she stirs something on the stove.

"Sure fucking did," I mutter. "And I'd like to kill him."

She shakes her head. "I'm sorry. Simon invited him without even asking me. Bracken just showed up. I guess they talked after the funeral and made up." She opens the oven, checks on the food, and turns back to me. "Do you want me to sprinkle some extra cayenne pepper on his food? Maybe dissolve a laxative in his drink? You know I have your back, girl."

"No, just stay by my side. Don't leave me alone with him. I'm sure Simon is going to try to pull some underhanded move to get us to talk about things."

"Got it."

"Hi, girls," my mom calls out, strolling into the kitchen. Her eyes go straight to me. "Did you invite Bracken?"

"Negative," I answer. I get up, pour a glass of wine, and chug it down. "Your other traitorous child did." I smack her side when I noticed her thin lips twitch into a smile. "It's not funny, Mother. I'm disowning him."

Her smile doesn't budge. "It's cute. He wants you to be happy."

I pour another glass of wine and snort. "Let's not even go there."

"Come on, sweetie. You're all older and more mature now. You need to talk to him."

"I wouldn't say *all* of us are more mature," Macy mutters with a laugh, resulting in me shooting her a dirty look. Her face turns serious. "As bad as I want to smack the cocky bastard, I agree with your mom. You need to talk to him. I'm not saying jump back in his bed or anything, but at least clear the air."

"That's a terrible idea," I answer.

"What's a terrible idea?" Annabelle asks, rushing into the kitchen with a doll in her hand. Her blond pigtails that topped off with bright pink bows bounce as she skips over to me and hugs my legs.

"Oh nothing," I say, wrapping her in my arms and kissing the top of her head.

"I like that nice guy out there," she says. "He's really funny."

I hold back the curse words on the tip of my tongue. He's trying to win my niece over now. The guy never did play fair.

* * *

I'm sitting on the top step of the front porch while everyone else is in the house. I'd been watching Annabelle show me her cartwheels but got ditched for bath time. I stayed behind, in need of fresh air. I look back when I hear the door squeak open and frown as Bracken takes a seat next to me.

Dinner was awkward, to say the least.

Everyone was apprehensive about Bracken and me. The conversation stayed along the lines of how everyone else's day went. I stayed quiet but was silently plotting out my revenge on Simon, who wouldn't stop throwing in hints that I needed to talk to Bracken.

He stretches out his legs and swings the beer bottle back and forth in his hand. "So what grade do you teach?" he asks.

"Seventh." My response is sharp, and I stare straight ahead.

"You were always good with kids."

Speaking of kids ...

I need to keep my mouth shut, but I can't.

"So where's yours?" I can't hold the question back any longer. My mind goes back to what I walked in on that day: the sobbing redhead, the pregnancy test, and the terror on his face when he saw me.

"She, uh ... had a miscarriage."

Damnit. Now I feel bad for bringing it up. This is why it's a bad idea for us to talk. Anything will blurt out of my mouth.

"I'm sorry," I whisper.

I know miscarriages can be hard. Macy and Simon have been trying for baby number two for a while now, and she's had two miscarriages. Neither one of them has taken the losses well. There's something hard about getting your hopes up and it all falling apart.

He lets out a long, deep breath. "Rachel was before you. I'd been having sex with her for about a month but didn't touch her after our first night together. She'd been blowing up my phone and showed up in hysterics that day, claiming she was pregnant and the baby was mine. She brought the test, which you saw. You came in at the same time the results showed up. I was in shock, terrified, and lost in the moment. I overreacted and was an asshole to you."

"That's for sure." I want to tell him what a pussy he was for letting Jasper be the one who ran after me, but I stay quiet.

"And I'm sorry for that. I know being overwhelmed isn't an excuse for my behavior, but I was. The whole situation with my dad and me, and Simon and his accident, and then losing you was tough. I was still trying to figure out how to make shit right, and then she showed up. The dream of working for my dad was gone after I found out about the affair, and now I needed to find a new way to support a kid. My life was a fucking mess. Rachel ended up miscarrying, and losing the baby was hard on us."

Wow. We both stay silent for a few minutes, looking at the colorful sunset.

"Are you still together?" I finally ask.

"No. We were never technically together. We'd agreed to co-parent, but after the miscarriage, we eventually lost contact. We touch base every now and then. She's married and has twin boys."

"That's good."

"What about you?"

I don't say anything. "Married? Dating? Kids?"

I shake my head.

"What about your engagement to Quinton?"

I finally look over at him with a raised brow. "Have you been stalking me?"

He fights back a smile. "You were engaged to an NFL player who signed a forty-million-dollar contract. You were all over the news as the perfect couple, attending your ESPY awards and all that shit. The football player and the teacher, you were America's Golden Couple. Yes, I have kept tabs on you, but it wasn't hard to find my information. All I had to do was look at a magazine in the checkout aisle at the grocery store."

"Perfect couple." I roll my eyes and snort. "Don't believe everything you read."

"So, you're not together anymore?"

I shake my head and take a swig of wine. "We tried to make it work. It was too complicated with his football, my job, everything. It was too much."

Quinton knew what happened with Bracken, and he knew Bracken had a place in my heart that he could never fill. There was also the problem of him being in the NFL. That involved lots of traveling and *lots* of jersey chasers. After the second *incident*, I handed him back the five-carat engagement ring.

"My dad left the dealerships to me." His statement is thick with emotion, and I can hear his guilt.

The fact that Randy left him the dealerships doesn't surprise me. I knew my mom didn't want them and felt like they belonged to Bracken.

"What are you going to do? Keep them? Sell them?"

He shrugs. "I'm trying to figure that out." He finishes off his beer. "I started a few dealerships with Jasper. They do pretty well, and I'm not sure this is where I want to be."

"Why not?"

"Because I don't know if I can stay in this town, live here, with you hating me. There's no fucking way I can know you're only a few miles down the road, so close I can throw a rock at your window, and not have you be mine. There's no way in hell I can be here and watch you be with another man. That will drive me up the wall. Why do you think I never came back?"

I wince. His words are like a stinging smack in the face, leaving a mark. "You said it years ago," I hiss. "You and me, we're a bad idea."

"I was a stupid fucking kid years ago who didn't know shit."

"Too much has happened." I run a hand through my hair. "Why now, Bracken? You show up five years later, after a tragedy, no less, and expect me to forget everything? You can't just snap your fingers and think I'll fall right back into your arms. It doesn't work that way. I'm not that young, naïve college freshman who's obsessed with you anymore. It's not that easy."

He turns me to face him. His eyes meet mine underneath the porch light. "Tell me what I have to do."

"There's nothing." I jump up from the step before I lose it. "It's too late."

"It's never too late," he says, looking up at me. "And I'll prove it to you."

twenty-nine

"WITH THE EXCEPTION OF INVENTORY, not much has changed," I say, walking alongside Pamela as we make our way through the showroom loaded with shiny new cars. We've already done a lap around the lot, and now it's time to talk specifics. I have to decide whether I want to take over or sell.

There are more cars on the lot than before, but other than that, everything is the same as the last time I was here—the holiday party with Nautica. I glance at the room where I'd taken her over the desk and fucked her. My dick stirs just thinking about it. The room is empty, and I know which office will be mine if I decide to stay.

"Randy thought the last remodel was enough," she tells me, leading me into an office with my dad's name on it.

I gulp. I'm not sure if I'll ever be able to take it off.

She takes a seat behind the desk while I shut the door.

"How are the numbers?" I ask, sliding my hands into my pockets.

Her lips form a proud smile. "The best they've been in years.

Most of our competitors have gone under after the recession. We're getting all their business."

"That's good to know." I gesture out the window to the showroom. "And you don't want this? This thing is a vault of money and success." She'd be dumb not to take this opportunity. It would set her up for life.

When I first found out she was fucking my dad, I'd been convinced she was a gold-digger who'd been playing my family from day one, waiting to sneak up on my dad and take his money. But I was a dumb kid. I know now that wasn't the case. She loved him, he loved her, and I'm an asshole for even thinking that.

She shrugs. "Car sales and running a company aren't necessarily my thing." She taps her fingernails against the desk. "Plus, I think it's rightfully yours. Your dad's plan for years was for you to take over. I'm giving both of you that."

"You have a house payment and bills. How are you planning to pay for that shit?"

"Randy left me with enough money to live a comfortable life, and I still have my job." The sound of her sliding open a drawer echoes through the room. I'm caught off guard when a set of keys come my way and fall into my lap. "So what do you say? Are you ready to be the CEO of Casey's Auto?"

I play with the keys in my hand. "I'll think about it." I don't want to sound like a dick, but I'm not sure about this.

"Are you not sure because of my daughter?"

I snort. "Am I that obvious?" *Do I look that damn desperate?*

"This might be hard to believe, but she's been waiting for you."

The keys almost fall from my hand. "What?"

"She's been waiting for you." She goes on before I have the chance to disagree. "I know what you're probably thinking. She was engaged to Quinton, but she wasn't planning on marrying him. She knew that. He knew that. I'm pretty sure anyone who knows her knew that. She was trying to force herself to move on, but every time he begged her to pick a date, she'd delay it."

"Maybe she just didn't want to get married. Trust me, she hates my guts."

She lightly laughs. "No, she doesn't. She's angry with you, but can you blame her?"

I shake my head.

"You finally let her in and then walked away when she was the most vulnerable, after promising you wouldn't hours before. My daughter is a stubborn woman. Getting her isn't going to be as easy this time around. You have to work for it, but the best things in life aren't easy."

"I know." I knew it'd be a challenge before I even got here. "But I can't commit to taking the dealership yet. If she denies me, I can't see her with another man. I'll have to leave town."

"Take the dealership. It will be harder for her to stay away if she knows you're here for good. If she sees you every day, she'll come around."

She has a point. I have to show Nautica there's no getting rid of me, and I'm not leaving again. She needs to know that she'll see my smiling face everywhere she goes.

"I'll take it," I say. "I'm staying."

She responds with a grin.

* * *

After checking in at the front office, I stroll down the locker-filled hallway and head straight toward the room number Pam gave me. The chances of her talking to me are higher here, considering she can't scream and kick my ass out without making a scene.

The classroom door is wide open. I take a step back and

stare at her for a few seconds. She's parked in front of her desk, concentrating hard on a stack of papers and marking them up.

I lightly knock. She frowns, the pen in her hand dropping when she notices me.

So far, not so good.

"You've got to be kidding me," she snarls, annoyed. "You're showing up *here* now."

I grin, holding up the greasy bag filled with cheeseburgers and fries, and walk in farther. "I brought you lunch."

She slides the chair out and pushes herself to her feet. My eyes stay on her as she sneaks past me to slam the door shut. She whips around to face me, her face red with anger, and rests her hands along her hips.

"This has to stop," she says. "You can't just show up at my job."

I toss the bag on the desk behind her. She lets out a gasp when I grab her hips and press her against the side of it.

"Why are you fighting this?" I ask.

She shivers in my hold as I run a hand across her warm cheek.

"Why are you running away from me?"

"I learned how to run away from the best," she spats, trying to pry my hands off, but I only tighten my hold.

"I'm sorry. I'll say it every day if that's what you want. Leaving you is the biggest regret of my life." I twist a long strand of her hair around my finger and fix my eyes on her. I lower my voice to an almost whisper. "Tell me what I have to do."

She lets out a breath. "It's irreparable."

My lips go to her mouth, slowly and carefully, and I press them against hers. I stay still, waiting on her reaction. She pushes into me and slides her tongue into my mouth. I suck on the tip as my hands travel down her back.

Her leg hitches around my waist as I grind into her roughly. A rush of air escapes her lips as I grab her ass and pull her harder into me.

"Irreparable my ass," I say, tearing myself away.

I have to stop before things go any farther. As hot as it sounds, I can't lean her over the desk and fuck her right here, right now. I don't feel like getting her fired or being arrested. I straighten out her skirt and give her a peck on the cheek. "Now that we know you're still fucking mine, let's eat. I'm starving."

I'm hungry for more than what's in the bag.

She snatches the sandwich from me and falls back down in the chair. "Asshole."

I grin.

Step one is complete.

I'm getting closer and closer.

* * *

It's official.

I'm now the owner of Casey Auto Sales.

I'm on a roller coaster of emotions. Growing up, I had this planned. Go to college, graduate, and take over the business, but I didn't think that was in the cards for me any longer. It's bittersweet.

I hit Nautica's name after leaving the attorney's office and send her a text. I probably look like some obsessive stalker showing up everywhere she is, but I don't give a shit. I'm going to fight for her like I should've done a long time ago. I have years to make up for. I'm not letting another day pass.

Me: What are your plans for dinner?

I think back to our texts when we were sneaking around. *Damn, I miss those days.*

My phone beeps with a response.

Nautica: Who is this?

I forgot I changed my number.

Me: The man you're in love with.

My response is pushing it, but that kiss in her classroom is giving me extra confidence.

Nautica: OMG, Channing Tatum?

Me: Funny. If I recall correctly, you choose to fuck me over watching him that night. Looks like I win.

A few minutes pass and I don't get a reply. Yeah, pushing it.

Me: Dinner? You have plans?

Nautica: No.

Me: My place or yours?

Nautica: What?

Me: Do you want to have dinner at my place, yours, or go out?

Nautica: Yours.

I send her my address.

Me: See you tonight at six.

* * *

I'm renting until I figure out what my game plan is. When I came here for the funeral, I paid for the first place that would let me in on a short notice without a lease. The two-bedroom apartment's rent is overpriced as hell, but the place is decent and came furnished.

I own a condo back home, but I plan to put it on the market. I also co-own a few dealerships with Jasper, but I'm considering letting him buy me out. They're up-and-coming, successful dealerships, but they're not anything like what my dad's are. His dealerships have had years in the making and a great reputation that people trust, which is hard to find in the auto industry.

Nautica sent me a text telling me she's on her way. I grab a lighter and start lighting the candles I bought at the grocery store earlier. I never thought I'd be a dude who buys candles when a chick comes over, but hey, shit happens.

My gaze keeps going to the door, and I grin when I finally hear the knock. She gives me a small smile when I answer it. I grab her hand and pull her inside.

She looks sexy as hell. Her dark hair is parted down the middle and pulled into a tight ponytail. A pink button-up blouse is tight around her tits. I lick my lips as my fingertips tingle with the urge to undo each button. My cock aches as I move my gaze down and eye her black skirt, imagining how easy it would be to slide it down to her ankles and slide inside her.

I shake my head in an attempt to stop my fantasies from running wild. I need to be good and keep my hands to myself ... for now, at least.

"Wow, this is a nice place," she says, looking around.

"Thanks," I say and clap my hands. "Dinner is almost ready. Can I get you a glass of wine?"

"Wine would be great, thanks." Her heels click against the floor as she follows me into the kitchen.

I pull out a stool for her to sit down before popping open a bottle of red wine. "How does chicken sound?"

Chicken is about the only thing I know how to cook, so it was either that or takeout. I thought it'd look better if I made something.

"Chicken sounds good." She takes a sip of wine before clearing her throat. "But first, I want to get straight to the point."

"Go for it." *Please don't be bad.*

"Why did you ask me to come here, Bracken? And why the

hell do you keep showing up everywhere I am? At my job, my house, and insisting I forgive you?"

I pour my own glass of wine. I knew I was going to have to start answering her questions sooner or later. "Because I want you to forgive me," I simply answer.

She dramatically throws her hands up in the air. "Fine, I forgive you. Happy? Does that honestly make you feel better?"

I shake my head. "Your acceptance doesn't mean shit if it's not real and you're not over it. Right now, when you see me, all you think about is how I hurt you. I fucking hate that. When you see me, I want you to smile. I want your day to brighten. I want you to see me as the man you love, not the one who hurt you."

"It's a little too late for that," she mutters, downing her glass and holding it out for a refill.

"It's never too late for shit."

I turn around to check the food and change the subject when I face her again. I'm waiting until the perfect time before I venture into deep territory.

Dinner is going by smooth so far. I've kept the conversation flowing, avoiding anything serious, and kept our glasses filled. She tells me about her students and how she started coaching the dance team. I tell her about how we started the dealerships, and she asks me how Jasper is doing.

Everything has been fine. There's been laughter and smiles, but I have a feeling it's about to change. I have to ask. The words have been on the tip of my tongue since I laid eyes on her at the funeral home and noticed the absence of Quinton and a ring.

"Was it just him?" I ask.

Her eyes meet mine from across the table. She tilts her head to the side as her eyebrows squish together. "What?"

"Was it just Quinton? Are you done with him? Is there anyone else?" I have to know if someone is standing in my way.

Her jaw flexes. I hit a nerve.

"Oh no," she mutters. "I'm not discussing my love life with you whatsoever."

"I need to know."

My throat goes thick at the thought of another man putting his hands on her—on what's mine. I have no damn right to be jealous. To be staking a claim. It's my fault, my own cowardice, for her running into the arms of another man. But I can't help it. There's still something between us – a spark that won't burn out. I can't move on from her.

She sighs as if giving up. "Yes, it was only Quinton. We were together for a few years. We broke up five months ago, and I've been too busy focusing on myself to worry about a man." Her face twists in annoyance. "But I'm not going to ask you that question because I'm sure there hasn't just been *one* other woman."

"You're right."

Her eyes widen at my honesty.

"I won't lie to you. I want us to be open and honest with each other." I slide my plate toward the center of the table and lean in closer. My elbows rest on the table as I lower my voice. "And do you want to know how I felt about all those nameless women?"

"Not particularly."

"Nothing. *Not shit.* I imagined they were you *every* single damn time. I haven't had anything like we had. Not a relationship, a date, nothing but one-night stands."

She claps her hands sarcastically. "Bravo, that's not surprising." She takes a sip of wine, swallowing it down slowly. "Why are we talking about this? Dinner was going well."

She doesn't see my confession like I do. Sure, I've given my dick to other women, but I've never handed over my heart. That means more to me.

"Do you still love him?"

She jerks back but doesn't answer me. A few seconds of silence pass before I can't take it anymore. I've never been a man of patience. Her back straightens when I slide out of my chair.

"Did you even love him?" I ask, stopping directly in front of her. "Or do you feel the same way as I do? That no one can replace our connection. Our love."

She scoots her chair out, gets up, and attempts to maneuver around me, but I grip her wrist, stopping her.

"I'm leaving," she snarls. "I agreed to dinner, not a fucking interrogation."

"No interrogation, just one question," I growl.

Only a few inches separate us. She's so close I can feel her heavy breaths against my cheek.

"Answer it. Answer my question, and I won't ask you another fucking thing," I continue.

I release her. She takes a step away from me.

"No," she replies.

"Answer my fucking question!"

"No."

"I'm right, aren't I? That's why you're trying to walk away— because you still have feelings for me."

Her face burns as she throws her arms out. "Yes, all right. Are you fucking happy now, asshole? Are you happy that you completely ruined love for me? Does it make you sleep better at night that no one else is capable of having my heart because you took it a long damn time ago?"

I can't help but grin. "Yes, it does."

She points at me. "I want to smack that smart-ass smile off your face."

"I want to kiss that cranky-ass look off yours."

She gapes at me and stumbles back. "That's ..."

"Romantic? Sexy as fuck?"

She lets out a huff. "Rude."

I chuckle. "How's this for rude?"

I slip my arm around her waist and jerk her forward. She doesn't struggle this time as she falls into me. No, she moves in closer, wanting more, and rocks her hips forward. I seethe, hissing in a breath, and push my growing erection against her.

Her skin is hot as I drag my hand up her shirt. My heart pounds harder as I unbutton it. I inch the sleeves down her arms and toss it on the floor. My nerves are spiraling as I take a step back and look at her in question, asking for permission. She nods, a faint smile on her lips, and I slowly ease the skirt down her legs. As bad as I want to rip it off and give it to her hard and rough, I hold back.

I have to take my time. This moment needs to last as long as possible.

My mouth waters as I take in the sight of her hard nipples underneath her white bra. I slowly trace my finger around one.

"We shouldn't be doing this," she says but doesn't move away.

I gently twist her nipple and chuckle, remembering our first time together. Our uncertainty, the apprehension, but we couldn't resist it. History is repeating itself. I'm not fighting it this time around.

"We should be doing this," I say, still playing with her breast. "We should because I love you – because I've loved you for years, even when I didn't even fucking know it myself. I loved you then. I love you now. I'll never stop loving you."

"What?" she stammers out.

I've never uttered those words to anyone other than my parents, but they should've been said a long damn time ago. Those three words are the only way I know how to express the feelings I have for her.

"You heard me. I'm in love with you, Nautica. That's what I've been trying to tell you since I've been back. That's why I've been begging you to forgive me because it's no fun having the person you love hate you."

I go still, waiting for her to say something back. *Anything.* Her lips slam shut, and she looks around the room. I'm not sure if I'm going to get a kiss ... or a kick in the balls.

I open my mouth to fix this so she won't leave, but her lips hitting mine stop me from doing shit.

Fuck yes. This is exactly what I'd been hoping for.

"Take me to your bed," she rasps out against my lips. "Show me. Show me how much you mean what you said."

I stand there, paralyzed, and run her words back through my mind before kissing her harder as reality kicks in. I taste delectable wine and tangerines as she slides her tongue into my mouth. I breathe in the sweet scent of flowers shooting up my nostrils.

I wrap my arms around her curvy waist and lift her. Her legs hook around my hips perfectly as I carry her to my bedroom. I clench my teeth, my dick getting harder as she grinds her pussy against me roughly.

I nudge the door open with my knees and carefully set her down on the bed. I back away, my footsteps heavy, and flip on the light.

I have to see this. I want to savor the moment of her being in my bed again.

"Wow." That's the only word I'm able to get out.

She props herself up on her elbow and signals for me to

come closer. I feel my dick getting harder as I do what I'm told. Her back presses against the mattress, her hair spread across a pillow, and I groan while joining her. A trembling moan escapes her throat, and her head falls to the side when I lean down and suck on the warmth of her neck.

"Yes," she whispers. "That feels so good."

I move south, and my lips go straight to her nipples as soon as I take off her bra. I suck hard, licking the tiny pebble, and travel my hand underneath her panties. Her skin is soft, her breaths shallow, and I grin when I find her clit.

She's so fucking wet.

I release her nipple and look up at her. She nods once before grinning. Her back arches when I plunge a single finger deep inside her.

"Shit," she cries out.

I add another finger, driving them in and out of her until she's crumbling underneath me. Her pussy soaks my fingers with her juices.

"I want you," she says, pushing me back and getting up on her knees. She makes a grab for my belt buckle. "I want you right now."

I lean back and allow her to undress me. She concentrates, clear determination on her face, as she unsnaps my jeans. They fall slack against my knees. Her eyes widen, and she licks her lips when my hard dick springs forth. She strokes me, causing my knees to buckle.

My shirt is the next to go. I shiver as her chilly hand runs down my chest, her fingernails lightly scraping along my skin.

"Holy shit," she says. I hold in a breath, uncertain if that's a good holy shit or a bad one. She traces the letters inked into my skin. "Is that *my* name?"

I nod, my eyes pinned to her hand.

It's a simple tattoo on the side of my chest. Seven letters in black, wrapped into the world of other tattoos, but it still stands out. I got it a few years back when I was wasted off my ass and feeling the blues about letting the girl I loved go. Jasper tried to stop me, but I told him to shut the fuck up.

She lets out a giggle as a soft blush rises along her cheeks. "I'm actually pretty flattered," she says. Her front tooth bites into her bottom lip. "As a matter of fact, I'm *really* flattered."

I grunt as I'm pushed back onto the bed. Her tight lips wrap around the head of my dick. I curse to the air, my balls aching, as she sucks hard before taking me in her mouth. She keeps a slow and steady pace, killing me.

"I'm about to bust," I croak out, but she doesn't hear me. Or she's ignoring me. I pull on her ponytail roughly.

She keeps ignoring me.

I pull harder.

She doesn't stop, but her eyes move up, meeting mine.

I gulp hard. "Don't let me bust in your mouth." I'm begging. "Don't let me off that easy. I need to be inside you."

She gives my dick one good final lick before pulling away. Her lips build into a slow grin. "Your wish is my command. Do you have a condom?"

"In the nightstand," I say.

I try to turn over to reach for it, but she stops me. My mouth waters as her naked body stretches across mine, and she opens up the drawer. She rips open the wrapper and carefully slides the condom over my cock. She slides her panties off. I seethe when she straddles my lap and slowly eases down onto my length. My hands clamp on her hips when she bucks forward.

Fuck. She feels so good.

I've missed this. I've missed her.

Our motions start slow, like we're getting used to each other again, and the old sparks start to flare back up. She picks up her pace, lifting herself up and falling down roughly.

"Fuck yes, baby," I grunt, throwing my head back. "You feel so good." I grip her hips tightly. "Did you miss this?"

She keeps fucking me, trying to avoid my question, but I don't let her.

"Did you miss this?" I repeat.

"Yes. I've missed this."

I allow her to start moving again. "I've missed you. I've missed everything about us."

She fucks me harder—like that confession set her on fire. She slams up and down on my cock. We're getting sweatier, more worked up, and we both cry out in release.

We're united again.

My girl is back in my arms, and I couldn't be happier. Now, I have to make sure she feels the same way.

thirty
NAUTICA

"SHIT! FUCK! SHIT!"

I jump out of bed, almost face-planting on the carpeted floor, and fumble around the foreign bedroom in search of my clothes.

This is not good.

Wine and stupid decisions are my story for last night.

"Good morning, babe," the sleepy voice behind me says cheerfully. I cringe, wishing I didn't wake him up.

I look back at the bed to find Bracken awake with his attention on me. He stretches out his arms and yawns loudly.

I snag my bra from the floor and put it on. I'll worry about the embarrassment of him seeing me rummaging around his bedroom naked later.

"I'm late," I answer. "I wasn't supposed to stay the night." *I especially* wasn't supposed to have sex with him. I scoop up my shirt. "I have to be at work." I look at the alarm clock on the nightstand next to him. "In an hour."

It's only a ten-minute drive from his place to mine, so that leaves me plenty of time to shower and get ready if I hurry.

"Do you need me to do anything for you?"

I pull up my skirt. "No."

He nods, but I can see the disappointment on his face. He wanted to save the day. "Don't start thinking too much today, okay?"

What the fuck does that mean? "What?"

"I know how you get in your head sometimes. You'll be sitting at your desk all day fighting with yourself on whether last night was a bad idea. Don't." I open my mouth to tell him he doesn't know shit, but he keeps talking. "Go home. Get ready for work. I'll meet you at your apartment in thirty minutes with breakfast."

I stand there and just at him. *How the hell does he expect me to respond to that?*

"Babe," he barks, breaking me away from my thoughts. "You better get going if you don't want to be late."

"Yeah ... right. I guess I'll talk to you later." I start to leave his bedroom.

"Wait."

I turn back to look at him. "What?"

A playful grin spreads across his face. "Where's my goodbye kiss?"

I let out a snort. "You've got to be kidding me?"

Our little late-night, drunken rendezvous was a one-time thing. I need to find the best approach to explain that to him, but it has to be later. I can't be late for work.

He points at his full lips. "Nope."

I *really* don't have the time for his shit. In order to prevent wasting any more time, I dramatically stomp around the bed and plant a kiss on his cheek. He throws his head back in laughter when I rush away before he has the chance to grab me.

"Oh, come on, babe," he says. "I had my mouth between your legs last night. You're really going to get shy on me now?"

I send him a wave. "See ya."

I have to get the hell out of here.

* * *

"We fucked."

"Well, good morning to you, too," Macy replies on the other line. "I figured something like that happened considering you didn't call me last night bitching about how bad he pissed you off."

I grabbed my phone as soon as I got in my car to call her. My confession had to be released. I need her to tell me what an idiot I am and to stay away from him.

"Big mistake. Big fucking mistake," I say.

She stays quiet for a few seconds. "Was it, though?"

"I'm sorry, but whose best friend are you? My traitor brother is getting into your head and causing you to turn against me, I see. We're the co-founders of the Bracken Hater's Club, remember?"

"No one is getting in my head. I'm only saying that you might want to give him a chance." Her words are rushed out, like she's afraid to say them. "I mean, you did have sex with him last night, and now you think the worst thing you can do is give him a chance to work things out? I think you should've thought about that before you let him fuck you."

"You're beginning to sound like my mother," I mutter.

"You're a smart girl. You knew the consequences of having sex with him. You knew it'd be more than a one-time screw to him."

"I was horny and in desperate need of a good lay."

"Oh, please. This town is packed with men who'd be up for the job. You went to him because you wanted him, not just a good lay."

"Your best friend card has been revoked. Call you later."

* * *

My fourth period class is clearing out when my phone rings. I snatch it from the drawer, expecting to see Bracken's name flashing across the screen since he's taken on the role of being my personal stalker lately. I frown and am pissed at myself for being disappointed when it's not.

Damnit. My vagina is already missing him.

As promised, he showed up at my apartment with a box full of donuts and coffee. He stopped me before I left and made a show of kissing me, adding a hint of tongue, and then sent me on my way. I thankfully arrived at work just before the bell rang.

This is starting to become a problem. It's harder to stay away from *this* Bracken—the one who wants a relationship with me—than it is with the one who kept fighting what we had. It's difficult to say no, harder to walk away, and more complicated to stop loving him.

I grab my phone and answer it. "Hello?"

"Hey sis," Simon says, his tone chirpy. "Are you at work?"

"Yes."

"We're having lunch today," he tells me matter-of-factly. "I'm on my way to the school now. Be there in five."

The line goes dead.

* * *

"So you and Bracken?" he asks.

We just sat down in a booth at our favorite Mexican restaurant and gave the waiter our order.

After recovering from his accident, Simon ended up going back to his job in the military for three more years before deciding to join the police force here. He wanted to be with his family more and watch his daughter grow up.

"There is no me and Bracken," I answer.

"Don't bullshit me. I heard you talking to Macy this morning about your little sleepover at his place last night."

I take a drink of water to get my reply in order. I'm going to kill Macy and her big-ass mouth. "Why does it seem like my life revolves around him now? That's all anybody asks me about." I give him a dirty look and flick the tip of my straw with my tongue. "No one asks me how my day is going, how my students are, or if I want an all-expenses-paid vacation. No, all you assholes ask me about is him and what's going on with us like it's the juiciest news in town."

He gives me a bright white smile. "Well, it kind of is."

I throw a napkin at him.

"But in all seriousness, we all want you to be happy."

I jerk back in my seat. "Are you kidding me?"

He shakes his head. "Do you not remember five years ago when you wanted to castrate him after you found out about us? Or how crushed I was when he left me at the worst possible time? Do you not remember how bad he hurt me?"

"The guy has made some dumbass mistakes, I know that, but he's owning up to them. He's planning on taking Casey's Auto so he can be here with you. He wants to settle down here *with you.*"

"But why now?" I ask with a frown. "And why are you suddenly so okay with this?"

"I'm older and more mature."

I snort.

"I'm not some guy who thinks he can control everything anymore. Bracken is a good guy. Sure, he's made some mistakes, but you can't fault him too much for it. He just lost someone really close to him. Do you remember how hard it was when we lost Dad?" I nod. It was the worst feeling in the world. "Can you imagine how fucking shitty you'd feel if you hadn't talked to him in years when he passed?"

I slam my eyes shut, feeling bad for Bracken. I know it has to be hard on him. It would be hard on anyone.

"He thought he'd have more time," Simon goes on. "When he lost his dad, it was like a reality check. He realized he couldn't keep waiting around until the perfect time came, or until he felt like enough time had passed for you not to hate him. He knows he needs to go for what he wants now before it's too late."

"He hurt me. You were in the ICU. I was broken, and what did he do? He turned around and walked away. I needed him there, but he didn't give a shit. I think it's time I do the same."

"You're not that cold-hearted. Give him a chance to make things right."

"Fine. I'll think about it, but you're paying the bill. You've put me through enough stress this week." He laughs when I give him a sarcastic smile.

This week has been a roller coaster. Craziness is following me around like a cloud. Something I wanted years ago is now sitting in the palm of my hand, but I'm not sure if I want it anymore.

Am I still in love with Bracken? Yes.

Do I trust him? No.

I can't figure out what's harder: telling him no, or giving him another chance and possibly getting hurt again.

thirty-one

NAUTICA

I TOSS my bag over my shoulder and head toward the apartment building that's becoming too familiar.

My mind has been choked with thoughts of Bracken nonstop since I woke up naked in his bed this morning. Hell, I've been thinking about him more in this past week than I have in years. I'd been slowly getting over him more with each day, but now all that hard work is deteriorating.

He texted and asked if I'd come over when I got off work. Another text followed, telling me to bring an overnight bag and cancel any plans I have for the weekend.

I replied with a no. He said yes. I said no.

And he won, considering I'm standing in front of his door waiting for myself to muster up the courage to knock.

We had sex last night—great sex—something I thought would never happen again. I'm waiting to wake up from this fervid dream.

I jump back when the door flies open before I have the chance to do shit. I look up to see Bracken's large frame standing in the doorway. His eyes are fixed directly on me as a smirk crawls across his lips.

"I saw you pull up from the window," he tells me. "I figured I'd help you out in case you got lost *or* tried to make a run for it."

I play with the strap of my bag. *Dammit, why does it seem like the man can always read my mind?*

"Nope, I was just ..." My words come out like a stutter. *Why am I so damn nervous?* I was vulnerable and naked in his bed last night, and now I can't even form a complete sentence?

"Deciding whether to bail on me?" he asks, taking the words out of my mouth.

"Yeah, pretty much."

He takes my bag, leads me into his place, and sets it down onto the carpeted floor next to another one.

"Are we going somewhere?" I ask.

He heads into the kitchen, opens up the fridge, and starts packing bottles of water into a cooler. "We sure are."

"Where?" I assumed he told me to pack an overnight bag because he wanted me to stay here—not go somewhere else.

"It's a surprise."

"Yeah ... I don't like surprises." I join him in the kitchen. "I'm not letting you take me to some unknown place to stay *overnight.*"

The old Nautica would've been game and excited for this, but not this one. No, I want no part in surprises from the man who crushed my heart.

"Well your surprise-hatin' ass is going to have to get over it."

"You're expecting me to be okay with you leading me to who the fuck knows where and stay the night without giving me any info? You've lost your damn mind. You asking me to bring a bag was pushing it, but this, it's outrageous."

"I sure am." He grabs my face and plants his lips on mine before I can stop him. "Trust me, we're going to have fun."

I need to pull away, but my feet are locked in place. My

mouth hovers back over his, and I can feel his harsh breaths kicking at my lips.

"I don't think you know what's fun to me anymore," I whisper.

He chuckles. "Oh babe, I can probably name a few things." I shiver as his tongue runs between my lips before he takes a step back.

I stay frozen while images of last night play out in my mind. I shut my eyes and can almost feel him inside me again. I blow out a breath, hoping to calm myself down. I don't want to leave. I want to push him down on the hardwood floor and take him right here, right now.

He's sucking me back into his world, faster and more intense than before, which means the hurt is going to be harder to get through this time around.

"Come on," he says.

I go stumbling forward, my mind still not straight, when he catches hold of my hand. I'm trying to keep up as he grabs our bags on the way out the door and guides us to the parking lot.

"This is me."

An oversized, red four-door truck beeps at the same time its lights flash. He releases my hand to open the passenger door.

"You always did have a thing for trucks," I mutter, jumping in.

He stops, standing next to my seat, and arches a brow. "Correct me if I'm wrong, babe, but so did you. Or at least the back seat of them." He winks, his upper lip twitching into a smile, while I glare at him.

I flinch when his hand runs along my thigh, right underneath the hem of my skirt.

"You need to loosen up before I find a much more entertaining way to get you to unwind. And trust me, we won't make it out of the parking lot if we do it my way."

He laughs when I push his hand off me.

"Fine," I say, making a show of moving around and pulling the seat belt across my body roughly. "I'm all loose. Now go away."

He keeps laughing as he shuts my door and tosses our bags in the back seat. "You're going to love this."

Dammit. I hope not.

* * *

"Oh hell no," I shriek, looking out the window in anguish. He's *so* wrong about me loving this. So damn wrong. "Turn this car around now, Bracken," I add, looking over at him.

He puts his truck in park and glances over at me in amusement. "Problem?" he questions.

"Yes, problem." I signal out the window. "This ... it isn't happening."

It's dark outside, and we've been on the road for nearly four hours. My anxiety increased with every passing mile about where the hell he was taking me. I'd been expecting something different, but definitely not this.

"Last time we were here you enjoyed it," he argues, unable to hold back his smile.

"Last time I was a dumbass," I correct. I cock my head to the side when he holds up two fingers.

"You have two options, babe. You can sleep out here or you can jump out and follow me into that nice, heated building."

"I'm not going in there with you, *period.*" I cross my arms. "Take me home."

He steps out of the car, ignoring me, and grabs our bags. My mouth falls open when he heads toward the entrance doors.

It's only thirty-five degrees out. I have no choice but to follow him.

I stand a few inches back, watching him as he approaches the woman standing behind the counter with a smile on her face.

"Reservation for Casey," he tells her, his voice husky.

I look around the place. I don't remember much about the lobby, but I'll never forget what happened in the room. The memory will forever be burned into my brain.

Why is he doing this?

Taking me down memory lane?

Why is he recreating all of the times I let him in?

When I was vulnerable?

He's trying to win me back with memories. Nothing is worse than having all of the reasons you loved someone who hurt you shoved in your face, suffocating you.

I stumble forward and follow him when he takes the key from the woman. I stay silent in the elevator and continue to let him show me the way.

"Can you believe they actually gave us the same room?" he asks, unlocking the door and going in. "I mean, what are the chances of that?"

I stop in the doorway, and a surge of memories powers through me. The beds, the TV, everything is the same. "You seriously remembered what room we were in?" I ask.

He drops our bags to grab my hand and pull me into the room. "Of course I did, babe. You might not believe me, but I remember everything about us." He sets me down on the bed. "Now, do you want to go to dinner or order room service?"

"Are we hanging out in here all night?"

"Hang out? Go to dinner? Make love to you until you forgive me?" He shrugs. "All of the above." He unzips his bag and drags out a bottle of wine. "I brought this." Next comes a stack of cheap plastic cups.

I snort. "Wow, you sure know how to wine and dine a chick."

He laughs, holding up the bottle. "Call me Mr. Romance. We can go somewhere, out to dinner, to a movie, but I thought hanging out here would be more entertaining. We can talk, work shit out, enjoy a drink in privacy."

I give him a faint smile. "That's actually perfect."

Minus the talking part. I will do anything to stop that from happening.

* * *

I pop the last bite of pizza crust in my mouth and put my plate on the nightstand. The hotel's room service menu was limited to grilled cheese and frozen cheeseburgers, so we decided to order a pizza and have it delivered to our room.

"So what's after this? Student-teacher porn?" I ask.

He looks at me from across the bed with a boyish smile. "Is that what you'd like to do next?" His eyes flash over to the remote. "That can easily be arranged."

The heat rising along my cheeks embarrasses me. Why does talking about sex with him make me feel so ... inept? I feel just as inexperienced as I was our first night.

"I ... uh ..." I stutter, trying to come up with the right words. "I was under the assumption that we were recreating the whole stranded in the blizzard night. Role playing ... or whatever."

I hold in a breath, watching him as he stands up and grabs the pizza box. He sets it down on the desk and comes back to me.

"We can do whatever you want, baby," he answers. His keen eyes sharpen on me. "But I think before we do anything we need to talk."

"Talk?" I repeat. That's the last thing I want to do right now.

Talking opens up too many bottles—too many emotions—too many memories of betrayal.

The room starts to grow hot as he stands only inches away from me. "Yes, talk. I want you to hear me out. I'm not touching you again, fucking you again, or doing anything until you listen to what I have to say. Then you tell me what I have to do to earn your trust and heart again."

I nod in response.

"I'm sorry," he goes on. "I'm so fucking sorry. I was young and dumb. I ran away from my problems, and I know this sounds stupid as fuck, but I thought I was helping you in the long run. I didn't want you to lose your family because of me."

That pisses me off. "That's bullshit. My family would've never left me. I don't understand why you would even think something like that."

He looks me straight in the eyes. "If Simon were to say, *"Pick me or him,"* who would you have chosen?"

I shrug.

"Back then, in the days when you wanted to be with me more than anything, who would you have chosen?"

I shrug again, even though I know the answer.

I would've chosen him over anything and anyone. I was so in love with him I would've walked through fire to get him to look at me. I would've stabbed a knife through my own foot for him to love me. As much as I love my family, the love-sick girl always chooses her heart over everything.

"Exactly," he says. "And my stupidity back then would've ruined us somehow. I was afraid you'd turn your back on them and then be left with nobody."

"You were also afraid of Simon."

"I wasn't afraid of Simon. I was more afraid of Simon wanting nothing to do with me. He was my best friend for years. I walked away because I didn't want to hear him say how much I betrayed him."

"People don't change. What makes you think I'm going to believe you won't walk away when something goes wrong this time?"

"I promise you I will never walk away. I'm here now, fighting for you, harder than I ever have. This is me telling you that no matter what happens between us, I'm here for good. Always. There's no running. We have a problem? We'll yell at each other, slam some doors, and make up. No bags will be packed. No calls ignored. I won't abandon you. I give you my word."

I blink, trying to hold back the tears surfacing. "Wow," I breathe out. "I wasn't expecting all of that."

"And I wasn't expecting to fall in love with my best friend's annoying ass little sister." He laughs when I slug him in the arm.

"Now I have a question for you."

We might as well get this shit over with. He looks down at me, causing my heart to beat faster.

I point next to me. "But first sit down, you're making me nervous."

I'm forced to scoot over when he plops down next to me. "Better?"

I nod, wrapping my arms around myself. "Better."

"Now what's your question?"

"The necklace."

"What about it?"

"What does it mean?" I've wanted to know this for years. I've racked my brain, going over our past conversations, but could never figure it out. *Step one.*

"I bought it before Simon found out about us and planned to give it to you for Christmas. After I left, I knew that wasn't an option, but I still wanted you to have it. I hoped it would let you know that even though we couldn't be together, what we had was real. I wanted to make sure you knew that you meant something to me – even when I was a mess."

"So you took the cowardly way out and mailed it? Did you honestly think I'd figure that out?"

"Yeah ... that probably wasn't that smartest thing I've ever done."

"What does it mean?" I press. I want to know more. "Step one?"

"It means moving forward. I was ready to take that first step with you. I was ready to step to the line of commitment and have a relationship. I wanted you as my own, and I wanted to be yours."

I look away from him, bitterness slowly crawling into me. "But then you chickened out. You took all of that energy to show me you were ready and then bailed like a wimp."

"Look at me." His voice is thick, but pleading.

I don't. I can't.

"I'm not going to answer shit if you can't even look at me."

Nervousness coils through me. I hesitate for a moment. This is venturing into too much uncharted territory. I slowly turn my head to look at him, noticing the look of concern on his face.

His hand locks onto mine. "You're right. I was a *wimp.*" He laughs at the term. "I was an immature guy who thought he knew everything and was afraid to deal with real life consequences. But that's not me anymore. I love you, Nautica. Forgive me for being a dumbass, for hurting you, for walking away like a damn coward. Give me another chance. Dig deep and drag out all of that love you once had for me."

His words. Damn, those words are like a firework charging through me, lighting me up with excitement, and burning me up with emotions.

I gulp and take a few breaths to get my words in order. "Okay," I say, with a nod. "I forgive you. I truly and deeply forgive you."

His face brightens up.

"I'm also trusting you with my heart again, and if you break it, there's no second chances."

He strokes my cheek. "You have my word." His lips form a grin, giving me chills. "Now we have another problem?"

"What?" I've had enough *talking* to last me for the next year.

"I haven't tasted you in years." I yelp as I'm dragged down the bed, and my legs are parted. "We need to rectify that."

I shiver at the feel of his cold hands against my stomach as he lifts up my top. My hips jolt forward when he skims a finger along my waistline before dipping it underneath the band of my skirt. My heart skips a beat when he unzips it, and I wriggle my ass to help him pull it down my legs.

"I've been dying to lick your pussy," he whispers, dragging my panties down. "It's been way too fucking long."

I squirm underneath him, waiting with anticipation as my blood boils. I've missed this. No one has gotten me off with only their tongue and fingers like Bracken has.

He cups me between my legs, his grip tight, and my hips buck forward. *Jesus.*

He skates the tip of his finger along my entrance teasingly— killing me. I let out a begging whimper. *God, I need this.*

"Have you been dying for the same thing?" he asks.

I can't say anything. All I'm focused on is his finger right there. *So close.* So damn close.

He toys with me more, adding another finger. "Nautica, answer me, baby."

I cry out when he pushes a finger inside me—just one. "If you want more," he goes on. "Tell me the truth. Tell me if you craved my fingers, my tongue, on your pussy every single night."

"Yes!" I cry out. I jump when he presses another finger into my heat. "God, yes!"

"Fuck yeah," he seethes.

His fingers thrust in and out of my entrance—hard, fast, and rough. It's agony, a delightful agony that I want to last forever. I rock back and forth against his hand. The agony turns into torture, and I jump when his tongue meets his fingers, lapping me up.

He's an expert at this—possessing me as he hits every spot I need him. His fingernails dig into my skin harder as I get closer. His tongue dives in deeper with each moan. I'm getting closer and closer until I shudder out my release.

"Fuck me," I breathe out frantically. "Fuck me now." I push myself up and start desperately undressing him.

Our arms and hands hit each other's as we try to do it quickly. I lie back as he drops his pants. His dick springs out, fully erect and ready for me. I lick my lips.

"Do you want me to wear a condom?" he asks, stroking his thick cock once.

I shake my head. "No. I just want you—raw, hard, no barrier."

My chest hitches as he crawls up my body. He plants his lips on mine as he slowly eases himself inside me. He makes me feel full, wanted, needed. I used to live for this feeling, and now it's mine again.

His mouth stays on mine, our tongues meeting, as he withdraws and sinks back into me. I gasp when he pulls back, his chest going straight, and starts to pound in and out of me.

I reach out and wipe away the tiny beads of sweat from his chest. "Why did you get my name?" I ask, feathering my fingers over it.

He looks down at me, his eyes hooded, but he doesn't stop fucking me. "Because I could never stop thinking about you." He slams into me with more force. "Because you're a part of me, and you needed to be etched into my skin."

I don't want to come yet. I want this feeling to last longer, but I can't help it. The way he's giving it to me, combined with how much I've missed this, is taking me over.

"I'm close," I tell him.

"Yes. Come all over my cock," he says, gaining more force with each thrust. He gives it to me harder, and I shudder out my release. He's still going, slamming into my body roughly until he fills me with his cum.

"I think that was better than the last time we were here," I say as he loses his weight on me.

"I think that was fucking amazing," he replies, kissing my forehead. "I can't wait to do this for the rest of my life."

thirty-two

NAUTICA

"ARE'NT WE GOING HOME?" I ask, noticing Bracken driving in the opposite direction of my house.

We're back in his truck after checking out of the hotel ten minutes ago. I still can't wrap my head around everything that happened in that hotel room. We made love two more times last night and had a shower quickie this morning. Being back in his arms, him being inside me, it all feels right again.

He glances over at me from the driver's side. "Have you always been this impatient?" he asks. "You used to be more game for my ideas. No questions asked."

"I used to be obsessed with you," I argue, halfway kidding. "You could've told me to chop off my pinky finger, and I would've asked you what tool you wanted me to do it with."

"So you're not obsessed with me anymore?"

I shrug. "Eh ... not really."

"Not really, huh? Sure didn't seem that way when you were begging me to fuck you harder this morning."

"I never said I wasn't obsessed with your cock."

"If you want to have my cock, we're a package deal. You have to take both of us. It's all or nothing."

I laugh and let out a dramatic sigh. "Fine, I guess I'll let you tag along."

"Glad you love being around me so much." He grabs my hand in his. "But I know you really love me as much as you love this dick, so no hard feelings."

I wish I could hide my blush. "And I know you love me just as much as you love my va-jay-jay."

"Damn straight. There's no denying that shit."

A few hours pass of small talk and listening to the radio before we pull up to a quaint restaurant a few miles from the KU campus. I used to come here all the time when Macy and I were in school.

More memories he's conjuring up.

"We drove all this way to go to lunch?" I ask, unbuckling my seat belt as my stomach growls. "You could've saved us a lot of time and money by going somewhere closer." I lose the warmth of his hand as he parks the truck.

"This is more than lunch," he replies. I raise a brow, asking for an explanation, but he only jumps from the truck and comes to my side.

"Elaborate," I demand, not in the mood for surprises, unless it's a puppy or something along those lines. A puppy would be nice—someone to spend the time with in case Bracken decides to skip town again.

"You'll see." He helps me out of the truck and leads me through the front door.

The place isn't busy. The hostess greets us with a bright smile before leading us to a backroom. Bracken's front bumps into my back when I stop in the doorway.

"Really?" I whisper, not bothering to turn around and look at him. I freeze up when his hands latch onto my waist. He stays silent while waiting for my next move.

I eye the scene in front of us. Jasper is sitting at a circular, family-style table with a woman who looks about my age parked next to him. Next to her is Bracken's mom. A man I don't recognize is in the chair to her left. Even though I want to turn around and run away, I clear my throat and head over to them, not wanting to be rude.

"Here comes trouble," Jasper sings as I get closer.

I stumble forward, almost tripping on my feet when I notice the baby cradled in his arms.

"It's nice to see you again." He hands the baby to the woman, stands, and hugs me.

I wrap my arms around him and smile. I haven't seen or talked to him since he ran after me at their apartment.

He points at the woman when I pull away. "This is my wife, Lanie," he says. The petite blonde throws me a shy wave, along with a smile. "And this is our daughter, Madeline."

I'm relieved Bracken told me about Jasper getting married and having a kid, or I would've fallen over in shock. I thought I'd never see the day he'd settle down. I guess it goes to show people really can change.

"Hi," I say, waving back. "It's nice to meet you, and your daughter is so precious."

I look at Bracken's mom, Lisa, who's grinning from ear to ear. I briefly saw her at Randy's funeral, but we didn't talk. I'm probably not her favorite person in the world, considering my mom was the knife that ripped apart her marriage.

I feel the heat of Bracken at my back again. He gives me a soft nudge, and I take that as my cue to sit down.

"Nautica, sweetie," Lisa says. "It's great seeing you again. You look so grown up and beautiful. My son has been telling me about your job and how well you're doing. I'm so proud of you."

"Thank you," I say, fidgeting in my seat.

She introduces me to her husband, and the waitress comes to take our order. I relax in my chair as I realize what's going on.

Bracken is walking me into the new life he has here with his mom and friends. He's showing me what I've been missing, what he's been doing.

Jasper picks up his fork when they bring us our food and uses it to signal back and forth between Bracken and me. "So are you two back together?" he asks.

I play with my napkin in my lap. Does he really have to start making things awkward?

"Honey," Lanie gasps, her eyes wide. She should know how outspoken her husband is by now.

"What?" Jasper asks with a shrug. "She knows I don't hold anything back. I want my best friend to be happy. I've watched him wallow around miserable for far too long." He points at me. "This chick right here, she's his happy factor, and I'm not letting him lose her again."

"I don't plan on it," Bracken says, taking my hand underneath the table. I shiver as his thumb runs along the top of it.

I look over at him and smile.

This is Bracken showing me his commitment.

I get it now.

thirty-three

BRACKEN

Six Months Later

"DON'T you think it's a little too soon?" Simon asks, looking at me from across the living room with a look of shock on his face. He definitely wasn't expecting this.

It's Wednesday night dinner. The women, along with Annabelle, are in the kitchen cooking and gossiping. I figured this would be the perfect time to ask his approval for something long overdue.

If this were five years ago, I wouldn't know how this conversation would go, but I'm feeling more confident now. I've been back in town, in their lives, for six months now, and it feels like I never left. I can't believe I'd been willing to give all of this up.

My eyes deadpan on him. "No," I answer.

"But it's only been months."

"No, it's been years in the making. You know that." I make eye contact with him. I want him to know I'm serious. "We took a break, sure, but that doesn't mean shit has changed about us, or how I feel."

He plays with the label on his beer, peeling off the edges. "You really have your mind made up, don't you? I want you to tell me right now you're serious, no bullshit."

"No bullshit. Nothing is changing. I'm not letting her go again," I say confidently.

He leans forward with a grin. "So how are you going to do it?"

I can't hold back my smile. "I have the perfect plan in mind. She's going to love it."

thirty-four
NAUTICA

"THIS IS our last performance before summer break," I tell the group of girls clad in bright-colored, sequined leotards standing in front of me. I clap my hands, and they nod their heads in response. I'm not sure if it's because the season is ending that they're so excited, but they can't seem to contain their smiles.

It's the last week of school. The year of teaching has come to a bittersweet end. I'm going to miss walking in and seeing a room full of students every morning, but I'm excited for my summer plans. Bracken and I are traveling through Europe for a month.

These past six months have been amazing. We're closer than we've ever been, and I mean *extremely* close. After weeks of insisting it was ridiculous for us to pay two rent payments, especially when I was staying at his place every night, I finally agreed to move in with him when the lease to my apartment expired two months ago. Over the past few weeks, we've been looking at houses for sale.

Buying a house together is a big step, but I think we're

there. In my heart, I believe Bracken is being honest when he tells me he's not going anywhere.

The girls form a single file line and strut out into the packed auditorium. I wave to the crowd as I make my way to my seat. I get comfortable, ready to see them perform the routine we've practiced dozens of times, but flinch when I hear the music start to play.

The wrong music.

I bound out of my seat and look around for the audio guy, but stop when I notice the girls start to dance like it's no big deal.

What the ...?

They're dancing a routine we've never practiced to Train's "*Marry Me.*"

I sit back down. There's no use making a scene and stopping them. My head starts to spin, and I hold my breath when they break away from each other, revealing him.

The spotlight lands on him standing in the middle of the stage wearing a full tuxedo. A bouquet of roses is clasped in one hand, and a microphone is in the other. His beard and hair are neatly trimmed, and a giant-ass smile is on his face.

I'm going to pass out. I know it.

The girls continue to dance around him, performing a beautiful routine until the music stops. They file out. The rest of the room seems to drown out. It's only him and me. He's the only thing on my mind.

The air is silent as he brings the microphone to his mouth. I look down and notice my hands are shaking.

"Hi everyone," Bracken says, waving. "Thank you for allowing me to interrupt, and thank you to the dance team for helping me make this perfect." He clears his throat, and his eyes search the crowd until he finds me. "There's something important that I need to do, and I feel like now is the perfect time. Nautica, can you come up here, please?"

"You go, girl!" Macy whispers, slapping my arm.

I can't move. I'm in shock. She gives me a helping push, and I rise from my chair. My steps are slow on my way to the stage.

I'm dreaming. I have to be dreaming.

He comes toward me, grabbing my hand to help me up the steps, and leads me to the center of the stage. I let out a breath of relief when I hear the ear-piercing sound of the microphone falling to the ground.

The crowd goes wild when he hands me the roses and drops down to one knee. My heart runs rampant. He reaches into his pocket and pulls out a black box.

This is happening. This is really happening.

"Marry me," he says, looking up at me with eager eyes.

I'm growing light-headed. *Please, don't let me pass out.*

"Marry me," he goes on. "Let me show you I'm not going anywhere." I gasp, my hand going to my mouth when he opens the lid. A gorgeous diamond ring sparkles underneath the bright lights. It's the most beautiful thing I've ever seen. I can faintly make out the crowd yelling behind us, but my attention is set on him.

I stand there, speechless, and he keeps going.

"Marry me, and I'll always be at your side. You and me." He grins arrogantly. "Marry me, and we'll find the perfect house, create an amazing family, and have a great life. So what do you say, Nautica Evans? Are you ready to keep me forever and make me the luckiest man alive? I promise you I'll make sure you're happy every single day."

I nod violently as tears fall down my face. "Yes. Yes!"

He pulls the ring out before grabbing my hand. "Be prepared to deal with my ass every morning and to give me a kiss every night."

"And possibly more," I say around a giggle. My voice is practically a squeak. I can't believe I'm making sexual innuendos during his marriage proposal. Thank God he dropped the microphone.

"And possibly more, *especially* in my truck."

"This can't be real life," I whisper.

"It's *our* real life. It's our love, and it's perfect."

The ring feels cold as he slips it on my finger. It fits perfectly.

Bracken Casey.

My brother's best friend.

My obsession.

My fiancé.

* * *

I'm lying in bed, relishing in the feel of the soft sheets against my back and Bracken's arm around my waist.

He proposed four hours ago, and I feel like I'm a princess in a dream. I finally slip the ring off my finger and take a good look at it. The princess cut diamond sparkles even in the dim light, and I eye the smaller cut diamonds wrapped around the band.

My heart flutters when I see it.

Engraved on the inside is: *The final step.*

also by charity ferrell

Beneath Our Faults

Pop Rock

Pretty and Reckless

Revive Me

Wild Thoughts

RISKY DUET

Risky

Worth The Risk